Tr... ...ad
on the flo... of his st... ...es that
there's ... know about the
residen...s o...

She needs to know more, for instance, about
Tim Baxter, who arrived at the scene of the
crime just minutes after Tracy...or was he
there already? And Tim Baxter is suddenly
paying a lot of attention to her...

So is Detective Inspector Neil Grant, whose
interest may not be purely professional—and
who fears, after a second mysterious death
that what Tracy doesn't know *could* kill her...

DESIGN FOR MURDER

DESIGN
FOR MURDER

by
Erica Quest

MAGNA PRINT BOOKS
Long Preston, North Yorkshire,
England.

British Library Cataloguing in Publication Data.

Quest, Erica
    Design for murder.
    I. Title
    823'.54 (F)

    ISBN 1-85057-753-6
    ISBN 1-85057-754-4 pbk

First Published in 1981

Copyright © 1981 by Doubleday & Co., Inc.

Published in Large Print 1990 by arrangement with the copyright
holder.

Printed and bound in Great Britain by
Redwood Press Limited, Melksham, Wiltshire.

CHAPTER 1

The first Wednesday in July seemed like winter, it was so cold and depressingly wet.

When I drove back from Cheltenham through the Cotswold countryside, heavy grey clouds were sagging down to fill every hollow of the hills with clammy mist. Wishing that I'd worn something warmer, I switched on the car radio and listened resentfully to a transatlantic report about the heat wave that was engulfing the U.S.A.

I reached the by-road for Steeple Haslop, and turned and dipped downhill through the beech-woods into the village. The wide main street, flanked on one side by the river, was rainswept and deserted. Yet the scattered cottages and early-Saxon church, all built of locally-quarried limestone which had mellowed over the centuries, still managed to exude a warm and friendly charm.

At Millpond Lane I was tempted to make the short diversion and stop off at my own cottage to change my clothes, but I was already later than I'd planned to be. As I turned in at the wrought-iron gates of Haslop Hall just up the hill beyond the village, the newscaster gave a time check. Twelve-fifteen, and I'd told Oliver to expect me at about eleven-thirty at our studio-cum-office-cum-workshop that adjoined his flat above the old Coach House. I'd been doing various things in Cheltenham, chief of which was selecting fabric samples for the Design Studio's latest commission—a complete new decor for Mrs Cynthia Fairford's drawing room at Dodford Old Rectory.

The long driveway curved through sheep-grazed parkland towards the ancient manor house, now half-obscured by drifting mist so that it was merely a looming grey outline. At the fork, I swung right and continued along a narrower, laurel-lined drive to the stable block. I drove through the archway beneath the clock-tower into the paved courtyard, and when I switched off the engine the country quiet was accentuated by the hiss and drip of rain. But then I heard a scurry of movement. Not, it seemed to me, of a horse stomping restlessly in its stall, but of hasty human footsteps.

Or was that only what I afterwards imagined it to have been?

As usual, I entered through the glazed door at the side of the Coach House which led by way of a boxed-in staircase directly up to the workshop. The door at the head of the stairs stood ajar, and as my eyes came level with the studio floor I saw, lying there, a huddled dark shape silhouetted against the light from the window. I bounded up the last few stairs. Then I stopped short, frozen with horror.

Oliver was lying between the desk and the table, on his side, with arms and legs splayed out. There was a deep wound in the back of his head. I crouched down and put out my hand to touch his cheek. Though it was still warm, the skin felt lifeless, and I knew with a terrible certainty that Oliver was dead.

A yard from his head, near the cabinet in which we stored rolled-up drawings, lay a heavy bronze statuette ten inches high that usually stood on top of the bookshelves...it was an African fertility-god which Oliver delighted in keeping on full view, largely, I suspected, to upset his father.

Instinctively I reached out and picked up the statuette. Then it occurred to me that I shouldn't be touching what was obviously the murder weapon and hastily dropped it. At the same moment I heard footsteps outside. The downstairs door opened and someone started to come up.

It was Tim Baxter, tall and ruggedly hand-some with a lean, bony face.

11

'Oh, hallo Tracy,' he began, with one of his attractive, lopsided smiles. 'I just wanted to...' Tim broke off as his gaze dropped to the body on the floor. 'Good God, what's happened?'

I shook my head helplessly, unable to speak. Tim went down on one knee and felt Oliver's pulse...needlessly.

'He's dead! What happened?' asked Tim a second time, rising to his feet.

'I...I just walked in a minute ago and found him...like this.'

Tim gave me a hard, steady stare, looking as if he wondered whether or not to believe me. Then his expression relaxed a bit.

'It can't have happened long ago,' he said. 'He's still warm.'

'I know.'

'You've touched him?'

I nodded. 'I wasn't sure if he really was dead.'

'Did you touch anything else?' Tim's glance went to the bronze statuette.

'Yes, I did pick up the statuette,' I admitted. 'But then I realised that I shouldn't have done and I dropped it again.'

'Too right you shouldn't have picked it up! With your fingerprints all over it, you'd have a hell of a lot of explaining to do.' He drew out his handkerchief and reached for the statuette.

He gave it a good wipe, careful not to touch the bloodied end, then he replaced it on the carpet.

'There, that's safer,' he said. 'Now we'd better call the police.'

'Safer for whom?' I burst out before I could stop myself. Horrifyingly, it had suddenly occurred to me that perhaps Tim Baxter was taking this chance, using this excuse, to wipe his *own* fingerprints off the murder weapon.

I watched Tim's brown eyes flare as he realised what I was thinking. To cover up, I said quickly, 'Don't you see, you might have wiped the murderer's fingerprints off too.'

Tim pressed his lips together, his expression thoughtful. 'I doubt he'd have been so careless as to leave any.'

'I might have disturbed him, though,' I pointed out. 'I thought I heard footsteps when I arrived.'

Tim had picked up the phone, but he paused and gave me a sharp look.

'Any idea who it was? Did you get a glimpse of him?'

I shook my head. 'I'm not even certain that I did hear anybody.'

But I *was* fairly certain. Could it have been Tim I thought wretchedly? If so, it was clever of him to return to the scene immediately after

13

my arrival. It would explain his presence in the neighbourhood of the Coach House if anyone else had chanced to see him, and it would account for any other fingerprints of his that might be found in the studio.

He said, 'Was it a burglar, do you think, whom Oliver surprised? Is anything missing, Tracy?'

I glanced round the room. Everything appeared to be in its usual place, with no sign that a search had been made. The hexagonal desk was untidy, but that was quite normal; Oliver always managed to create chaos when he opened the morning's mail. There was a catalogue beside the telephone, a roll of Sellotape, a selection of coloured ball-points, and...

'It doesn't look like it,' I said. 'Not that there was anything much to steal in here—nothing particularly valuable, I mean. And Oliver never carried a great deal of money on him. He preferred to use his credit cards.'

'He's still wearing his wristwatch, I see, and a signet ring.' Tim was fiddling with some of the loose papers on the desk, and I said uneasily, 'You shouldn't move anything, you know. The police will expect to find things exactly as they were.'

I'd left myself wide open to a comeback from Tim about *me* having picked up the statuette,

14

but he just nodded and dropped the sheet of paper he was holding. Then he dialled 999.

'Oliver's father will have to be told,' I said. 'Shall I go?'

'No, I'll do it.' I didn't care for the thought of being left here on my own with the body. 'I'll go now, before the police arrive.'

I slipped out while Tim was talking into the phone. Once through the courtyard archway I turned left along an avenue of horse chestnut trees, which a month ago had looked magnificent with their creamy white blossom but today dripped forlornly in the rain. Then out into the open across neat lawns and well-tended rosebeds towards the house.

Originally built in the fifteenth century, Haslop Hall had been added to over the centuries before architecture became an exact science. It was a happy hotpotch of pitched roofs and pointed gables, of leaning chimneys and mullioned windows eccentrically positioned. It was listed as a landmark building, as it well deserved to be.

I entered beneath the Gothic-arched portal and tugged the iron bell handle. After quite a wait my summons was answered by Grainger. He and his wife ran the domestic side of Haslop Hall, with the aid of a couple of daily women, one of whom doubled for Oliver in his flat.

15

'Miss Yorke. Good afternoon.'

'Is Sir Robert at home, please?'

'I think not, miss. I believe that the master is still out around the estate somewhere. But if you will take a seat, I will enquire. Or Lady Medway, perhaps, if she is now returned from riding?'

It wouldn't be right for me to break this dreadful news via Oliver's stepmother, his father's glamorous third wife. 'No, it must be Sir Robert himself. There's been an accident, you see. I mean...'

Grainger gave me a startled look from beneath his bushy eyebrows. He was a short, thickset man, and stood with his arms hanging, palms forward, which gave him an almost apelike appearance.

'An accident, miss? To Mr Oliver?'

'Please,' I begged, 'try to find Sir Robert for me. He must be told immediately.'

I waited impatiently in the Great Hall, not sitting down but pacing around beneath the gilt-framed portraits of the family ancestors; which Oliver, to annoy his father, insisted on calling the Rogue's Gallery. It was nearly five minutes before a door leading from the rear regions opened and a tall, stooped figure came through.

Sir Robert Medway, though nudging sixty,

16

was still a handsome man; but problems with his heart had marked him, leaving him a shade too spare of flesh. An unhealthy pallor showed from under his summer tan. He came to me, his walking stick hooked over an arm, still wearing a dripping raincoat and muddy Wellingtons, careless of the mess he was making on the priceless Bokharan carpet.

'Miss Yorke, what is this I hear from Grainger? How badly is Oliver hurt? Where is he?'

I felt terribly nervous, wondering how he would take the news. He and Oliver had been at loggerheads for years; but even so, Oliver was his son and heir, and it would be a terrible shock.

'I'm dreadfully sorry, Sir Robert, but I'm afraid that Oliver is...dead.'

'Dead?' A tremor shook his body. 'What happened, girl? Tell me!'

'I don't really know what happened, Sir Robert. I've been in Cheltenham all morning, and I arrived at the studio just a few minutes ago and found Oliver lying on the floor. He'd been hit on the head.' Better to get it over with in one go. 'There seems no doubt, I'm afraid, that he was murdered.'

'Murdered! Oh, my God! Are the police there? Is that what they say?'

'No. We've called the police, of course, but

they haven't arrived yet. There hasn't been time.'

'We?' he asked sharply.

'Tim Baxter happened to come by...just after me. He's waiting there with Oliver.'

Sir Robert's agony showed in the look he turned on me. Usually so self-assured and confident, he seemed lost now.

'Hadn't we better get over there?' I suggested gently.

'Yes...yes, you're right.' With a visible effort he pulled himself upright and marched towards the outer door. Grainger suddenly appeared from nowhere and I guessed that he'd been eavesdropping.

'Sir Robert, what am I to tell her ladyship when she arrives back?' he enquired anxiously.

Sir Robert's stick fell to the floor, and Grainger dived to retrieve it. 'Tell Lady Medway nothing. I'll be back as soon as I can.'

Sir Robert was already through the front door and heading across the lawn towards the chestnut avenue, taking such long loping strides with the aid of his stick that I had to trot to keep up with him. It was raining again, and the slashing raindrops struck through my cotton blouse and made me shiver.

Sir Robert halted so abruptly that I almost bumped into him.

'I've always dreaded something like this,' he muttered, but I knew he was speaking more to himself than to me. 'I've always feared that Oliver would come to a bad end.'

'It was scarcely Oliver's fault if he surprised a thief...' These were meant as soothing words, spoken without thought. I didn't believe in any thief; I just wanted, if I could, to lessen Sir Robert's pain.

The police hadn't wasted any time getting here. One of their cars was drawn up in the courtyard, and a uniformed constable was leaning through the open door talking on the radio. As we approached, another car drove in and I recognised the driver.

Neil Grant was hardly more than an acquaintance nowadays, but at one time we'd belonged to the same crowd of young people and I'd known him fairly well. At thirty, he was already something of a high flyer in the police force.

Seeing Neil, the uniformed constable broke off his radio conversation and said, 'Through that door, sir, and up the stairs. You'll find P.C Bailey there.'

'Right, Bill.' Neil flickered me a glance of acknowledgement but spoke first to Sir Robert. 'I'm Detective Inspector Grant, sir, stationed at Gilchester. Er...this is a dreadful business.

Have you just arrived on the scene yourself, sir?'

'That's right. Miss, er...' Sir Robert stared at me, my name momentarily escaping him.

'Miss Yorke,' Neil prompted.

'Yes, Miss Yorke. She came to the Hall to tell me what had happened. I came straight over, of course.'

Neil nodded. 'Perhaps we'd better go inside.'

He led the way up the narrow staircase. Another constable was standing beside Oliver's body writing in his notebook. Tim was near the window, his hands thrust into the pockets of his denim jacket. He met my eyes briefly and gave me a faint smile.

'The doctor's on his way, sir,' the constable said.

'Good.' Neil acknowledged Tim with a brief nod, then turned to me. 'It was you who discovered the body, I understand?'

'That's right.' The memory of that first awful moment caught me in the throat.

'Not the two of you together?'

'No,' said Tim. 'I arrived a minute or two after Tracy.'

'And what time was this exactly?'

'I'm not sure of the exact time,' I said. 'But it was just a minute or so before we phoned for you.'

'Right. The call came through at twelve

twenty-seven precisely, so you made the discovery between twelve-twenty and twelve-twenty-five. Would that be a correct estimate?'

'I should think so.'

With a brisk nod, Neil turned his attention to the body on the floor. Not wanting to look, I watched Sir Robert instead. He had put his hands to his face and was rocking backwards and forwards. I was afraid that he might faint, and I stepped a little closer, ready to support him.

'I think you should sit down, sir,' said Neil, noticing. 'In another room, perhaps?' He glanced in my direction. 'I expect you know your way around here. Could you find somewhere comfortable for Sir Robert to wait? And you'—his gesture included Tim—'must hang around, too. I'll need to talk to each of you in a few minutes.'

Tim went towards the inner door that led into the flat, holding it open while I persuaded Sir Robert to come with me. I led him along the corridor, where new windows overlooking the courtyard had been cut in the old stone walls of the Coach House, and into Oliver's big lounge, where I sat him down on the sofa. Then I went to the drinks cupboard and poured him a measure of brandy, glancing enquiringly at Tim.

21

'Not for me,' he said, shaking his head.

It was quiet in here, and deeply luxurious. Oliver had always been boldly imaginative with colour, and his most daring combinations invariably seemed to work. Here he had used peach walls, a burnt-orange shag-pile carpet, and the upholstery and window drapes were in swirling designs of violet and green. There were bright cushions scattered around, small glass-topped tables, and a number of modern paintings. The wide windows gave a view across the grounds of Haslop Hall towards the trout stream that meandered through the valley bottom. Beyond the perimeter wall, the wooded Cotswold landscape undulated into the misty distance.

Tim was pacing restlessly, surveying the room with a contempt he didn't trouble to conceal. Very faintly, we could hear a murmur of voices coming from the studio. The police doctor would have arrived, I guessed, and a photographer and all the other specialists needed at the scene of a murder. I had heard at least five more cars arriving in the courtyard.

Though I encouraged Sir Robert to drink the brandy, it did nothing to restore his colour. He seemed on the verge of collapse, and I was scared that he might suffer another heart attack at any moment. I wished it were possible to make this less of an ordeal for him, but what could I say? What could I do? I sat beside him on the sofa and waited helplessly. Tim continued to prowl about, sometimes stopping to stare out of the window. Water draining off the roof was gurgling round a bend in the guttering, and every now and then a gust of wind spattered droplets against the glass panes.

Presently there came sounds of activity in the corridor outside. Probably they were searching the flat for signs of an intruder. Sir Robert seemed not to have heard, but Tim and I glanced expectantly at the heavy mahogany door, whose panels were carved in a riotous tumble of cupids. Oliver had acquired this door in payment of some obscure debt when a house built as a love-nest by a rich Victorian roué was being demolished. I watched the gilt handle dip slowly, and the door opened to reveal P.C Bailey.

'Er, excuse me, Miss Yorke, but the Inspector would be obliged if you'd step along to see him. He's in the dining room.'

As I rose to my feet I glanced anxiously at the crumpled figure of Sir Robert. I heard Tim say gruffly in answer to the unspoken doubt in my mind, 'I'll be here with him, Tracy. Don't worry.'

CHAPTER 2

Neil Grant was alone in the dining room. He had established himself in the carver's chair at the head of the oval mahogany table, a large notepad set out in front of him. He rose as I was shown in, and motioned me to the chair opposite him where I faced the light from the window.

'How is Sir Robert taking it?' he enquired.

'As you would expect for someone with a bad heart. It's been a terrible shock.'

'I'll try not to keep him too long,' Neil said, as he sat down again and took out a pen, 'but I wanted to talk to you first. I imagine you were as close to Oliver Medway as anybody.'

There was a suggestion in his tone that I didn't like, and I reacted sharply. 'Just what do you mean by that?'

Neil regarded me blandly, his sandy eyebrows raised. 'You were his assistant, weren't you? Working alongside him day after day, you must have come to know the man pretty well.'

'I suppose that's true,' I acknowledged, only partly mollified.

'Right. Well now, there is no obvious sign that a search was made—either of the body itself or of the premises. So can we, for the moment, rule out theft as a motive for the killing? You haven't noticed anything missing?'

'No, nothing is missing as far as I can see. At least, not in the studio. I can't really say about here in the flat.' I glanced around me quickly. 'It doesn't look as if anything's been stolen, and the lounge seemed the same as usual when I was in there just now.'

'You're familiar with the flat, are you?' he said, making a few rapid notes in shorthand.

'Well, yes. Oliver never tried to keep the studio entirely separate from his flat, so I've been in here quite often. Most days, though, I only came through to make coffee in the kitchen, and to use the bathroom.'

'I see.' Neil nodded. 'Can you think of anything that has occurred recently, anything at all, that might help throw light on Oliver Medway's death?'

I shook my head. 'I don't think so.'

'Was he behaving in any way out of character? Did he appear to be worried or anxious lately? Had he been involved in any quarrels or disputes?'

I didn't quite know what to say. Oliver had carried a chip on his shoulder for being denied

25

what he regarded as his birthright. He thought that by now his father should have allowed him a major share in managing the estate, and he bitterly resented the fact that Sir Robert, despite his ill health, still insisted on absolute autonomy. But a reasonably satisfactory *modus vivendi* seemed to have been found; at least their relationship wasn't actively hostile.

There were Oliver's complicated involvements with women, of course. Mrs Cynthia Fairford was the latest, but as far as I knew they were still at the stage of sweetness and light. The commission we'd recently landed for redoing the drawing room of her home was largely an excuse for Oliver to make frequent and protracted calls at the Old Rectory. When I'd pointed this out to him, he'd grinned back unashamedly. 'Nice for me; good for business.' There was a lot about Oliver that I disapproved of, but he never gave his clients short change. Although he'd had no formal training in interior design, he'd had a flair for it. And in the fifteen months I'd been working with him I'd learnt an enormous amount.

I answered Neil's question decisively. 'No, I can't think of anything significant. Oliver has been acting much the same as always. He was in a perfectly cheerful mood when I last saw him.'

'Which was when?'

'Yesterday evening, about six-thirty. I was staying a bit late—working on an estimate—but Oliver had a date and he went through to the flat to get ready.'

'Do you know who his date was with?'

'No, he didn't tell me and I didn't ask. Oliver went out almost every evening.'

Neil's grey eyes flickered. 'With you, some-times?'

'Yes, as a matter of fact,' I said, letting him see how much I resented his tone. 'Once in a while Oliver would take me out to dinner.'

'How often is once in a while?'

I shrugged. 'Maybe every couple of months.'

'You didn't go out with him more often?'

'No. Well, not in the evenings.'

'When else, then?' he persisted.

'We often went to see clients together, of course,' I said irritably. 'Apart from that, I used to ride with Oliver.'

'Ride with him?'

'Horses. Sir Robert still keeps a few in the stables here, and they have to be exercised. So Oliver and I often used to go out for an hour or so when we'd finished work for the day.'

'And afterwards?'

'Afterwards,' I said coldly, 'I would go home, and Oliver would go out wherever it was

27

he was going that evening.'

For several moments Neil remained silent while he brought his shorthand notes up to date. When he next spoke it was on a new tack, and his tone was so chillingly formal that it shook me.

'Now, Miss Yorke, I want you to tell me exactly what happened this morning. How you came to discover Oliver Medway's body.'

Miss Yorke! Okay, so Neil Grant and I had never been really close friends, but in the days before I'd gone off to art school in London to study design I'd often met up with him at discos, in coffee bars, at the Gilchester Lido in the summer, and cosy pubs of a winter evening.

'I spent most of the morning in Cheltenham,' I began, controlling my annoyance. 'On business, I went there straight from home.'

'You still live at your aunt's place in the village?' he asked.

'That's right. Honeysuckle Cottage in Millpond Lane. Aunt Verity left it to me when she died eighteen months ago.'

Neil nodded.

'I had arranged to join Oliver at the studio at about eleven-thirty. But I was behind schedule and didn't arrive until a quarter past twelve.'

'What delayed you?'

'I don't really know. I mean, I had several things to do and the time just slipped by. When I did get here I found Oliver exactly as you've seen.'

'So what did you do then?'

'Well, as we explained to you in the studio, Tim Baxter turned up a minute or two later. He dialled 999 while I went over to the Hall to tell Sir Robert.'

'You say that Baxter "turned up." Were you expecting him?'

'No.'

'Why had he come, then?'

'He didn't get around to telling me. I suggest that you ask Tim yourself.'

'Oh, I will. Does he often drop in at your studio?'

'No,' I said, and added, 'not often.'

Neil seized on my slight hesitation. 'Has he in fact ever come before?'

'Oh yes.' He had done once, I remembered. Not to see Oliver or me, though, but because someone in the estate office had told him that he'd find the agent, Ralph Ebborn, with us.

'How did Baxter and Medway get on with each other?' asked Neil. 'Were they friends?'

'Not exactly friends,' I hedged.

'What would you call them, then?'

29

'Well, acquaintances, I guess. I suppose you know that Tim runs a small vineyard here on the estate?'

'So I'd heard.' Neil made a few more notes, then sat back in his chair. 'That's all you can tell me, then? There's nothing you'd like to add at this stage?'

'How d'you mean?'

His frown contradicted his patient tone. 'Did you happen to touch anything in the studio this morning? The body, perhaps?'

I shivered slightly. 'I did just touch Oliver's cheek.'

'Why did you do that?'

'To see if he was still alive, I suppose. I hardly know what I thought, when I found him like that. It was such a shock. The light wasn't very good, and I hadn't properly seen the...the terrible wound at the back of his head.'

That all went down in the notepad.

'It rather looks,' he said, 'as if Mr Medway was killed only minutes before you arrived. Yet you saw or heard nothing that might help us?'

I flushed as I suddenly remembered what I'd intended to report at once. 'As a matter of fact, just as I was getting out of my car, I did hear something...'

'Describe the sound. Where did it come

from, which direction?'

'I didn't really think about it at the time, but it was like someone hurrying down the other staircase.'

'The one that goes directly down from this flat?'

'Yes.'

'But that staircase leads into the courtyard, too,' he observed. 'So wouldn't you have seen whoever it was as they emerged from the door?'

'I would already have been inside by then, coming up the stairs to the studio.'

Neil raised his eyebrows. 'You didn't feel there was any need to investigate?'

'No, why should I have? I just thought that it was someone who'd been to see Oliver.'

'A man or a woman, would you say from the footsteps?'

I thought for a moment. 'Honestly, I've no idea.'

'That's a pity. Now, I'd like you to tell me about the bronze statuette. I assume it belonged to the victim?'

'Yes. Oliver used to keep it on top of those bookshelves by the drawing table.'

'A rather bizarre object to have on open view, isn't it?'

Actually, I agreed. Oliver had bought the thing a couple of months ago from the bric-abrac and souvenir shop in the village, and he'd chosen to display it in the most prominent position he could find. I'd told him it was childish to get such perverse pleasure out of shocking people. But Oliver had only laughed, and asked how anybody could object to such a splendid example of primitive art.

'It was a bit of harmless amusement, that's all.'

This time Neil raised just one eyebrow; otherwise his squarish face remained maddeningly impassive.

'Did you touch the statuette at all?'

That jolted me, and I parried, 'Whatever makes you think I might have done?'

'We've checked it for fingerprints and there aren't any. It's been wiped clean.'

I remembered Tim's comment, and said, 'Wouldn't the murderer have been careful to wipe it?'

'That's what I'm trying to establish. The position of the bloodstains it left on the carpet indicates that it was picked up from the floor more than once.'

'Oh.'

'So why not tell me?' he suggested in a suddenly gentle voice.

'As a matter of fact I did pick it up,' I admitted uneasily. 'I don't know why...just

32

instinct, I suppose. But I realised I shouldn't have done so the moment it was in my hand, and dropped it again. Then I thought that my fingerprints would only confuse the issue, so I wiped them off.'

'What with?'

I stared at him. 'Er...my handkerchief.'

'Show it to me, please.'

Reluctantly, I opened my shoulderbag. The only hanky in there was still smooth and folded as I'd taken it from the drawer this morning, and I tried to crumple it a bit as I drew it out.

Neil didn't even bother to take it from me. He merely remarked dryly, 'Try again, Miss Yorke.'

'It...it must have been something else, I suppose.'

'Are you sure it wasn't some*one* else? Someone else who did the wiping?'

I was too confused to answer, and after a moment Neil urged me, 'Don't make it worse than you've already done. It was Baxter, wasn't it? He's the only person who could have wiped the statuette *after* you picked it up, if it wasn't you yourself.'

I shrugged. 'Why ask me then, if you already know the answer?'

'Did you see Baxter do it?'

'Of course.'

'You didn't try to stop him?'

'He'd done it before I properly realised. Look,' I rushed on, 'Tim wasn't thinking, that's all. He didn't mean any harm, he was just trying to protect me from any misunderstanding on the part of the police.'

Neil's grey eyes challenged me. 'What is your relationship with Baxter?'

'There isn't a relationship,' I said in a stony voice. 'I know Tim about as well—or as little— as I know you.'

'Hasn't the possibility occurred to you,' Neil enquired imperturbably, 'that it might have been someone else's prints he was trying to remove from the weapon? His own, for instance?'

I felt the cold hand of fear press down on me and I found myself blustering in Tim's defence.

'Look, it's Tim Baxter we're talking about. You've known him most of your life. You went to school together, remember? And now you're making these foul suggestions...'

'I'm only asking questions.'

'Loaded questions.'

'It seems they need to be, to get you to admit the truth,' he said, still unruffled. 'Now there's one other thing, Miss Yorke. I want you

34

to give me a run-down of your movements in Cheltenham this morning. What time did you leave home?'

Struggling to keep my patience, I said, 'It must have been just after nine. It was nine-fifteen when I parked in my usual spot behind the Queen's Hotel.'

'And then where? In detail, please.'

'The first thing I did was to call in at an antique dealer's, Morrison and Fletcher, to look at a Bohemian crystal chandelier that Mr Fletcher thought might interest us for a room Oliver and I are replanning—*were* replanning,' I amended. 'Anyway, the instant I saw the chandelier I knew it wasn't right. But I stopped and chatted a bit with Mr Fletcher, and he offered me a cup of coffee. I suppose I left him soon after ten.'

Writing, Neil gestured for me to continue. It all seemed rather pointless to me. If I was a suspect, surely the only relevant factor was the time at which I left my last port of call.

'I had an appointment at ten-thirty with an importer of Italian silk brocades,' I went on, 'and...'

'Where was that?' he cut in.

I gave the address, and Neil made a calculating face.

'It wouldn't have taken you nearly half an

35

hour to get there from Morrison and Fletcher's, even on foot.'

'On the way I called in at the jeweller's to leave my watch for repair,' I explained. 'Havillands.'

'I see. Go on.'

'Well, I suppose I spent half an hour or so looking at the selection of brocades, and picking out a few samples to show the client.'

'That brings you to about eleven o'clock.'

'I spent a little while window shopping along the Promenade.'

'So what time did you finally leave Cheltenham?'

'I don't really know. But it must have been about a quarter-to-twelve, because it was twelve-fifteen when I turned in at the main gates here.'

'How do you know that so precisely, without your watch?'

'I heard a time check on the radio.'

'What else did you hear? What was the programme?'

I had to think before I remembered. 'Oh yes, there was a report from America about the heat wave.'

Neil took it all down. Then he got to his feet.

'That's all for the moment, Miss Yorke. Please wait in the other room, I may want to see you again after I've talked to the others.'

Holding the door for me, he told the constable to fetch Mr Baxter. I had no time to do more than give Tim a warning glance as he was called out of the lounge and I went back in...a warning he probably couldn't interpret. I felt guilty, as if I'd somehow betrayed him by admitting that he'd wiped the statuette. And yet...I was hopelessly confused about Tim Baxter.

Lady Medway had joined her husband. She'd been riding in the rain, and was less than her usual immaculate self. I later discovered that she had seen the police cars when returning her horse to the stables, and had learned about Oliver then. More than twenty years younger than her husband, Diana Medway was nearly forty, but this was the first time I'd seen her look anything like her age. There was a haunted expression in her violet-blue eyes, and her creamy complexion looked sallow now.

'What did the police inspector want to know?' she asked brusquely as the door closed behind Tim.

I said with a shrug, 'Oh, just preliminary questions—about how I found Oliver and so on.'

She shuddered. 'They brought me in through

the flat so that I shouldn't (to) see the body.'

Sir Robert glanced up and muttered something incoherent. It seemed to me that his wife was being curiously insensitive to his feelings. Surely there was some kind of comfort that Lady Medway could offer her husband? But they sat far apart on the sofa, two separate individuals; there almost seemed a hostility between them.

'Have the police formed any theories yet?' she continued. 'About who can have done it?'

I thrust aside Neil's obvious suspicions—and my own—about Tim, and shook my head. 'It's too soon for that, I imagine. They'll keep an open mind until they've finished questioning everyone who's even remotely connected with Oliver.'

Diana Medway glanced swifly at her husband and I saw a look flash between them. But it was gone too quickly for me to read its meaning. Then she turned to me again.

'They won't want to question *me*, surely,' she protested in an offended voice. 'It's so degrading. What do they think I could possibly tell them?'

'The police are always very thorough in a murder case, Lady Medway, they have to be. I think you should be prepared to be questioned.'

She looked away, staring with unfocussed eyes at the polished-copper fire canopy, while her slender fingers nervously pinched up the damp fabric of her riding breeches into tiny creases. The three of us lapsed into an uneasy silence, like patients in a doctor's waiting room.

Tim didn't return to the lounge. We only knew that he had left when Neil himself opened the door and asked if Sir Robert would give him a few minutes. He then glanced at me.

'I don't think we need keep you here any longer, Miss Yorke. You'll want to have some lunch, no doubt. So if you'll let P.C Bailey take your fingerprints, you're free to go. I'll be in touch with you again later.'

I hesitated for a moment when the two men had gone out, unsure whether I ought to leave Lady Medway on her own. But I doubted that she had any desire for my company. We'd never liked each other. Although she'd only been a minor actress before she became Sir Robert's third wife, that didn't stop her from treating me as an insignificant person.

On the way out I gave them my fingerprints—a messy business—then left the Coach House by the staircase from the flat. By now the courtyard was filled with police vehicles. I had to manoeuvre my Fiesta back and forth to extricate it from the tangle.

I felt at a bit of a loss. I still couldn't quite grasp the fact that Oliver, who'd always lived life right up to the hilt, was dead.

The prospect of going home to an empty cottage and being alone with my thoughts was decidedly unappealing. I considered going to the Trout Inn for a ploughman's lunch, or the cafe on the Gilchester Road for a hot snack. But news of the murder would have got around by now, and I was afraid that I'd be the centre of morbid curiosity. Anyway, I wasn't really hungry and I badly wanted to know the outcome of Tim's interview with Neil. The way Tim had beetled off straight away suggested that he wasn't any too pleased with me.

So instead of leaving the Haslop Hall grounds by the main gates, I swung round and headed for the exit by the Home Farm. Turning left, I took the lane which skirted the rounded hillock known locally as the Pudding Basin.

A rustic sign swinging on a chain marked the entrance to Tim's vineyard, Cotswold Vintage. This was a thirty-acre site of south-sloping land which he had claimed (and he seemed to be proving himself correct) would be absolutely ideal for the cultivation of wine grapes.

I turned in and followed a rising, muddy track, on either side of which was row after dead-straight row of vines, all neatly trained on support wires. Bearing to the left, I drove past some new winery buildings and in a moment reached the comfortable, ranch-style bungalow. Fortunately for Tim, the bungalow had become vacant just about the time he was granted use of the vineyard land by Sir Robert. It had been occupied by Ralph Ebborn and his wife; they had decided that the bungalow which went with his job as agent was too isolated, and instead had bought a Queen Anne house in the village.

It was raining too hard by now for anyone to be working outside, and there was no sign of Tim or his two assistants. But when I rang the bell, Tim came to the door.

'Oh, it's you,' he greeted me ungraciously.

'Why did you shoot off like that without so much as a word?' I demanded. 'I was wondering how things went for you with Neil Grant?'

'As if you didn't know!' But at least he stood aside to let me in out of the rain.

'Look,' I said, 'if you're thinking that I told Neil about you wiping off my fingerprints, you're dead wrong! What I told him was that I'd done it myself. But he somehow guessed that it wasn't me and insisted on seeing my handkerchief. So then he figured out that it must have been you. I'm sorry, but there it is!'

Tim's expression softened marginally, and he turned and led the way to the kitchen. There was a heavenly aroma of beef casserole, and it was clear that I'd caught him just as he was serving up his belated lunch. A table in the window was spread with a checked cloth and all laid ready.

'Don't worry, I won't stay a moment,' I said apologetically, and added, 'You certainly do yourself well.'

He grinned wryly. 'If it was left to me, I'd have bread and cheese. This is Mavis Price's doing...you know, I expect, that her husband, George, works here at the vineyard? So Mavis comes in and does for me each morning, and to her mind that includes providing a good hot nourishing midday meal for the poor helpless bachelor.'

'Very cosy.'

'You'd better have some too,' Tim said, taking off the casserole lid and prodding the contents with a spoon. 'There's plenty. She always makes enough for a troop of Boy Scouts.'

I shook my head. 'No thanks.'

'You've eaten already?'

'No, but I'm not hungry.' That wasn't true anymore, though. The tantalising aroma had restored my appetite. Fortunately, Tim brushed my refusal aside.

'Don't be silly, Tracy, you've got to eat,' he said, and immediately started to lay up a second place.

So I sat down, murmuring thanks. Tim poured out another large glass of his own product—the dry, tangy white wine that was beginning to make a name for itself. I'd tasted it once or twice before, and found it very good.

'Well, what did Neil Grant have to say to you?' I asked, as we both dug into our food.

'He grilled me as though he was the F.B.I and I was suspect number one.'

With very good reason, I thought unhappily. But I didn't believe it, *couldn't* believe it. Would I be sitting here with Tim, calmly sharing his lunch, if I seriously considered it possible that he was a murderer? This might have been a ridiculous, backwards kind of logic, but I wanted to trust my instincts about Tim. There was something about him that had always appealed to me.

'Neil made *me* feel like that too,' I said, with an attempt at a smile. 'Perhaps it's his usual technique. Perhaps it'll be the same for everyone else he interviews.'

'Think so?' Tim moodily toyed with his glass, swishing the pale wine around. 'He won't be short of suspects, I'm sure.'

'Why do you say that?'

43

'Wouldn't you agree that Oliver Medway was the sort of man who made enemies?'

'Oh, I don't know. With most people he was charming.'

'With women, you mean. But he could be a good deal less than charming when it came to men. He had a vicious way of putting people down, with that bloody superior manner of his.'

I couldn't honestly refute that. On a couple of occasions recently I'd felt embarrassed by Oliver's behaviour. Once, when an order of silk-flocked wallpaper had been delivered a roll short and he'd phoned the supplier to complain; and then at a client's house, when an electrician had misread his wiring instructions. Each time Oliver was witheringly sarcastic, not content with an apology and a promise to put the matter right forthwith. Trivial errors, but he'd reacted out of all proportion. And only last week he had roasted Billy Moon, the stable-hand, simply because the old man had for once forgotten to get the horses saddled up for our ride.

Tim was continuing. 'And don't forget, Tracy, that charmers have a way of leaving a trail of wreckage in their wake. How many women around these parts must have come to hate Oliver Medway? Not to mention all the husbands and jealous boyfriends. How many of them must have felt like having a go at him?'

'But surely not to the extent of killing him?'

'It doesn't have to have been premeditated murder,' Tim argued. 'Can't you imagine it...a man goes to the Coach House intending to warn Medway off, but gets provoked by that sneering air of superiority he put on. My God, it would be the easiest thing in the world to snatch up the nearest heavy object and bash him with it.'

'If you're right,' I said, 'the police won't be long in finding out who did it.'

'Why do you say that?' he asked quickly.

'Well, if it was a sudden fit of rage, the killer probably won't have covered his tracks any too well. In fact,' I couldn't help adding, 'by now they might already have discovered who it was, if you hadn't wiped off those fingerprints.'

The angry look on Tim's face made me wish I hadn't been so blunt, but then he shrugged and said, 'I suppose it was a damn fool thing to do. It seemed like a good idea at the time, though.'

'Why?' I demanded, but not too aggressively.

Tim looked down at his plate, pushing the food around with his fork.

'It's hard to say now. I suppose I thought

45

of all the probing questions you'd have to face about your relationship with Medway. It seemed simpler all round just to get rid of your fingerprints.'

Damn him! Tim seemed to take it for granted that I'd been sleeping with Oliver, just as Neil Grant had—and probably everyone else in the entire neighbourhood. Would he ever believe me if I told him the truth, that the 'relationship' had been purely platonic?

'Supposing it really was me who killed Oliver?' I said, flinging it out as a challenge.

His glance shot up to meet mine questioningly. Then he said slowly, 'But it wasn't, Tracy.'

'How can you be so positive?' There was only one answer to that: Tim could only know for certain that I was innocent if he himself had killed Oliver.

Perhaps Tim had seen that, too. He said— evasively, it seemed to me—'I just don't believe that you'd be capable of doing a thing like that, Tracy.'

'I wish the police shared your touching faith in me!'

We continued eating in silence for a bit. Then Tim asked abruptly, 'Will you keep the Design Studio going?'

'I don't see how I can,' I said. 'I couldn't

expect Sir Robert to let me have the Coach House premises virtually rent free, as he did for Oliver. Besides, what would I do for money? You have to be prepared to allow very long credit in this sort of business. Clients expect it.

'And I'm not really sure that I've got the necessary experience yet. It was different for Oliver. He was untrained, but his imagination sometimes used to leave me gasping with admiration.'

'So what exactly was your role in the set-up?'

'Well, it was up to me to translate Oliver's brilliant but nebulous ideas into reality. The reason I got this job was Sir Robert's insistence, before he agreed to finance the enterprise, that Oliver engage an assistant level-headed enough to keep his feet in contact with the ground.'

'And you,' Tim enquired, 'are level-headed?'

'I like to think so.'

'Was it level-headed to pick up that statuette?'

I put my fork down. 'I thought we'd finished with that subject.'

'I'm sorry,' he said mildly. 'Have some more wine.'

'No, I'd better be going. Thanks for the meal.'

'Won't you at least have some coffee?'

47

'No, I don't think so,' I said, and stood up.

At the door Tim's eyes sought mine, holding them captive for a moment. 'I'll see you, Tracy?'

'Yes, I'll be around...for a while, at least.'

CHAPTER 3

The rain clouds had cleared away in the night and the sunny morning seemed to mock my mood. I couldn't banish the feeling of unreality I'd woken with after a night of bad dreams; the peculiar feeling of numbness. Even now, a part of me still couldn't accept the fact that Oliver was dead.

In a way, I had been closer to Oliver since Aunt Verity died than I'd been to anybody; at least, he'd played a bigger part in my life than anyone else. So it was no wonder that his death left me feeling bereft. He had the kind of personality that was intoxicating. Every job we undertook he charged at head-on (though his enthusiasm never lasted for very long), and somehow he managed to make every working day seem exciting.

To add to my grief, I had to face the fact that I was now without a job.

While I was having breakfast the phone rang several times, as it had done all last evening. Friends of my schooldays whom I'd picked up with again after coming back to Steeple Haslop were calling to express their sympathy. And naturally—I didn't really blame them—they wanted to discuss the details of the murder. It was the biggest thing to have happened in this sleepy corner of the world for an age. There were also two or three calls from newspaper reporters, but these I gave short shrift.

After I'd cleared the dishes I retreated to the walled back garden, and began in a desultory way to nip off a few dead heads of marigolds and sweet williams. Then I sat on the swing that hung from a bough of the old pear tree.

Wandering on again, I found myself at the door of Aunt Verity's workshop, a spacious, stone-walled building she had designed herself. Light flooded in through big windows set high in the walls on three sides, and there was a skylight overhead. There were no eye-level windows, because she said they would be distracting. But on fine summer days she cheated by unbolting the bottom of the double doors and leaving them both open to the garden.

As always, the moment I stepped inside I felt a sense of closeness with my aunt. Everything was as she had left it when she became too ill to sculpt any longer. I wasn't preserving it as a sort of shrine, it was just that I kept postponing the task of clearing it out. Somehow that seemed such a final step.

Like my aunt herself, the place was thoroughly workmanlike, without any frills. A massive bench was set about three feet from the rear wall, with racks of tools behind it...mallets and chisels, rasps, and an electric polishing machine. Small sculptures and a number of models of her bigger pieces were ranged around on shelving, and in the centre of the floor was a great block of pink Cotswold alabaster mounted on a wooden plinth, with a platform to enable Aunt Verity to reach the top. This piece was to be the figure of Hebe, the goddess of youth, planned to stand in the entrance foyer of Gilchester's grand new youth centre. But it had scarcely been more than roughed out, the only detailed work done being on the head.

A great bronze gong stood in one corner, a trophy my aunt had brought back from a Far East trip. I tapped the hammered surface with my fingertips and listened to the faint shiver of sound.

It occurred to me suddenly that maybe I could set up on my own account in the interior-design business, using the workshop as my studio. But tempting though this was, I knew that as a practical possibility it just wouldn't work. I hadn't got the finances to carry me through the first few years while I built a reputation. No, I'd have to find myself a job—and that meant selling up and moving away from Steeple Haslop.

I heard a voice calling from the garden, and it was Mrs Sparrow. Ten-thirty already. Elsie Sparrow was an inheritance from my aunt and came in for a couple of hours two mornings a week. She needed the money, and although I didn't really need her (and couldn't really afford her) I hadn't the heart to tell her to stop coming.

'It must have been quite horrible for you, dearie,' she began in an awestruck voice. 'Fancy walking up them stairs and finding the body all smothered in blood like that.'

'Yes, it was a dreadful shock,' I admitted.

We returned to the cottage and I made coffee, resigned to having a chat with her. When I'd given all the details I intended to give and parried a number of artfully-angled questions, Mrs Sparrow kept the conversation going by remarking darkly, 'Mind you, I'm not a bit surprised that your Mr Medway came to a sticky end, the way he used to carry on. My Fred says that many's the time on his early milk round he's seen that red sports car of Mr Medway's parked where it had no business to be parked. Fred could tell a tale or two, if he'd a mind, about the goings-on round here.'

'If Mr Sparrow knows anything that could be relevant to Mr Medway's death,' I pointed out sternly, 'then he should go to the police about it.'

The suggestion startled her.

'Let them find out for theirselves,' she said, and stood up to begin work. 'That's what they're paid for. Nobody in their right mind goes running to the coppers—you never know what you might be letting yourself in for.'

On an impulse, partly to get away from Elsie Sparrow, I decided to go to the Coach House, though I more than half expected to be refused admittance. Still, they might at least allow me to collect any mail.

The thought of going back to the studio, of trying to work in the room where Oliver had been killed, was something I dreaded. But I couldn't avoid it; there was so much I would have to clear up. So the sooner the better, I argued to myself. It was like falling off a horse, and getting straight back on again before you lost your nerve completely.

To my surprise the courtyard was empty of cars. I glimpsed old Billy Moon sweeping out the stable, but he drew back quickly as if not wanting to be noticed.

As I let myself in I felt a curious sensation

of reliving yesterday. I felt almost convinced that I was going to be confronted with Oliver's body stretched out on the floor. It took every ounce of willpower to make myself climb the stairs.

There had been several letters on the mat downstairs, and a small package which contained the samples of gold tassels I'd sent for a week ago. Everything seemed unreal—as if nothing to do with me—and I just wanted to turn tail and run. It had been a mad idea to come to the studio this morning. I realised for the first time that someone around here— probably someone whom I knew personally— was a murderer. The thought made me feel sick with panic.

Yet I felt duty bound to stay and do my best to clear things up. Commissioned jobs couldn't be abandoned half done, and there were all kinds of loose ends to be tied off. I could hardly press Sir Robert for instructions, at least for the next day or two, so in the meantime it was up to me to do my best.

In cases where we were still at the early planning stage, there was little problem. The clients could merely be informed that the Design Studio was regretfully unable to complete the job, and I could recommend another firm of interior designers to take over. I mentally put these aside for the moment, as well as the jobs in which there were just a few bits and pieces to be finished off.

I was left with three undertakings which presented a real headache. Oliver had planned a dramatic revamp for the consulting rooms of a fashionable chiropractor in Cheltenham, and work was due to begin next week—the timing here had been an important factor in the contract. Then there was the new grill-room extension of the Golden Peacock restaurant over towards Stow-in-the-Wold, where the decorators were already in—almost finished, in fact—but it looked as if there was going to be a delay with delivery of the specially woven peacock-motif carpet. And there was Myddleton Manor in the nearby village of Haslop St John where Lady Chorley was having an expensive kitchen installed. At present the old kitchen and dairy had been stripped to a bare shell awaiting the laying of cork flooring and the arrival of cabinets and cupboards, ovens and hobs, fridge and freezer and dishwasher, and everything would need chasing up to be fitted ready for use in time for Lord and Lady Chorley's return from their holiday.

I also made a note of Mrs Cynthia Fairford at Dodford Old Rectory. Her new drawing room was still only a preliminary design on paper, but considering the lady's special relationship with Oliver it seemed to me that some tactful handling was called for.

I heard the sound of a car entering the courtyard, then there were footsteps on the stairs. It was Neil Grant.

'Hallo, Tracy! I dropped in at Honeysuckle Cottage just now, and your cleaning woman told me that I'd find you here.'

'Tracy?' I asked. 'Whatever happened to "Miss Yorke"?'

'Police business has to be conducted with a certain formality. You ought to appreciate that.'

'And isn't this police business now?'

'Well, yes. But I wanted to have an off-the-record chat with you about the general set-up here, to give me a better all-round picture.'

I shrugged, and gestured him to one of the comfortable red leather chairs. 'What is it you want to know?'

'You went straight to see Baxter after leaving here yesterday?'

'Are you asking me or telling me?' I said coldly.

'What I want to know, Tracy, is *why?*'

'Is it a crime?' I demanded. 'I just wanted to talk to Tim.'

'What about? Were you comparing notes?'

56

'Would that be so surprising, after all those questions you threw at us?'

Neil looked exasperated. 'Surely you can see that I've got to ask questions. It's the only way I can eliminate people from suspicion.'

'And are Tim and I now eliminated?'

He didn't answer that. Instead he shot off in a new direction. 'Tracy, how the devil did you come to be associated with a man like Oliver Medway?'

I didn't care for what he'd said, and I particularly didn't like the implication behind it.

'You may be interested to know,' I told him frostily, 'that working alongside Oliver Medway was an enormously valuable experience. He was one of the most talented men I've ever met...almost a genius.'

'He was lots of other, less admirable things, too,' Neil retorted.

'Such as?'

'For a start, he was pathologically promiscuous. People say that he couldn't keep his hands off any attractive woman who happened to cross his path.'

'So?'

'So, it could be relevant to his murder.' Neil eased a finger round the leather strap of his wristwatch, and glowered at me. 'Don't try and tell me that he never made a pass at you, Tracy.

I wouldn't believe you.'

'Then I won't.'

'Does that mean he did?'

'Oh, for God's sake!' I exploded. 'As you said, Oliver couldn't keep his hands off women. The first day I joined him he was trying it on with me.'

'And?'

I held back an impulse to scream out confirmation of what he obviously believed. Wasn't his big luxurious bed handy, only two rooms along from the studio?

I said in a furious voice, 'It was always strictly business between Oliver and me. I insisted on that. I couldn't possibly have worked with him otherwise.'

'I see.' It was as if the tempo suddenly changed, Neil once again becoming the brisk police inspector. 'I want you to make a list of every contact of Oliver Medway's you can think of.'

'Business contacts, you mean?'

'And personal. I gather that the two were closely interlinked. Did he keep a diary? We didn't find anything.'

'I can't imagine Oliver keeping a diary,' I said. 'Except the one over there by the phone for appointments.'

'We've looked through that already. There seems nothing much to interest us.' Neil glanced around as if for inspiration. 'Well, I'll leave you to get on with that list, while I have another look round the flat.'

He disappeared through the communicating door and I set about noting down names and addresses. To aid my memory, I looked up the correspondence files and account books. All the while I could hear the sound of doors opening and closing next door. When after a good half hour Neil came back, he started to give the studio a thorough inspection too, checking the titles on the bookshelves, then sitting at Oliver's desk and going through the drawers.

'I thought all that would have been done yesterday,' I said, finding the silence between us a bit creepy.

'It was,' said Neil, 'and very thoroughly. But whenever possible I like to have a quiet, uninterrupted browse without an audience.'

'Does that mean you'd like me to make myself scarce?'

'Oh, I wasn't including you, Tracy.' He gave me a rueful grin, which suddenly made him more human. 'When you've gained a certain reputation for being an astute detective, it's important to maintain the image—especially when your Chief Superintendent has entrusted you with a murder investigation. In the presence of other policemen I have to be seen sizing up situations in an instant. Making shrewd assessments and judgments. It wouldn't do at all for anyone to see Neil Grant lost for a lead.'

'And you're lost in this case?'

Neil let his glance rest on me until I felt uncomfortable.

'Put it this way, Tracy...there are too many leads, too many possibilities. Nothing stands out as obvious.'

'From your line of questioning yesterday,' I said dryly, 'I was under the impression that you thought it all very obvious.'

He shook his head and sighed. 'Like most people, you've got altogether the wrong idea of police work. Too much television, I suppose. Brilliant leaps of deduction hardly ever come into it. We have to rely on painstakingly collecting and sifting facts and opinions. Fitting them together and trying to discern a pattern.'

'Like a jigsaw puzzle,' I suggested, unoriginally.

'Exactly. And up to now I've scarcely got more than two or three pieces slotted together.'

'So you don't really believe that it was Tim Baxter?' I asked.

'Do you?' he shot back at me.

'Of course not!'

'You seem very positive.'

'I just know it wasn't Tim,' I said stubbornly,

trying to convince myself as much as him.

Neil settled himself more comfortably in Oliver's chair, stretching out his legs.

'Tell me about Baxter. He went off to horticultural college or whatever, I think, about the same time I joined the police. I'd heard that he lost both his parents, but that he'd returned to the neighbourhood. How did he come to start a vineyard here?'

'The way I understand it, Tim first got hooked on the idea while he was on holiday in France, as a student. Then when he came home after college, he spotted that piece of south-facing land on the slopes of the Pudding Basin, and realised that it was an ideal spot for grape cultivation. It seems that Sir Robert didn't object when Tim approached him, but Tim needed his help in financing the scheme, too. You see, there would be no crops while the vines established themselves—three years, I think it takes. Anyhow, he managed to talk Sir Robert into letting him have a go. Unluckily, though, Tim's first vintage was a terrible flop because of bad weather, but this past year things have picked up, and it now looks as if the vineyard will pay off.'

'Where did you get all this information? From Baxter himself?'

'No. I told you, I don't know him all that

well. It's just common knowledge that I've picked up from various people—including Oliver, I suppose.'

'I see. What was Medway's attitude towards Baxter and the vineyard?'

'He wasn't very happy about it, actually,' I said, minimising Oliver's many scathing comments.

I might have guessed that Neil would jump in on that.

'Shouldn't Medway have been pleased, once he saw that the gamble was going to pay off? If the vineyard is doing well and the Haslop Hall estate has a stake in the profits, he must surely have benefitted?'

'Not really, because his father kept him on a very tight rein.' I thought it necessary to add, 'Oliver wasn't very good with money—it tended to run through his fingers.' This could have competed for the understatement of the year.

'But the success of the vineyard would still have been to his advantage,' Neil persisted, 'I mean, when he eventually took over the estate himself.'

'Yes, but that might not have been for ages. Sir Robert is only about sixty. I know he's got a bad heart, but he's not the sort of man to give in to ill-health.'

'One would rather expect,' said Neil, slowly

and thoughtfully, 'that in a landed family like this, the son would be involved in the estate's management. Wasn't Oliver Medway interested?'

'Oliver *was* brought in for a time after he finished at university some years ago, but I gather that he and his father were constantly at loggerheads.'

'So what happened?'

'Sir Robert arranged for him to join his stockbroker's firm in London. But that didn't work out either, and Oliver drifted from one job to another, coming home in between times. Meanwhile, Sir Robert's second wife died, and he married for the third time.'

'That's the present Lady Medway?'

'Yes. She wanted changes made at the Hall, and Oliver came up with some brilliant ideas. Everyone realised suddenly that he'd got a real flair for interior design. So that was how the studio got started.'

Neil got up from the desk and strolled to the window, standing there with his fingertips resting on the sill, staring out.

'There's another son, isn't there?'

'A stepson, actually,' I said, 'but Sebastian has also been legally adopted. You see, he was only about three years old when his mother became Sir Robert's second wife. Sebastian is much younger than Oliver, of course; he's still up at Oxford.'

'I presume that he will inherit now, when the time comes?'

'I imagine so.'

'What's he like? I've not met him yet.'

I shrugged. 'I've only met Sebastian a couple of times, so I don't really know him. But he struck me as being very different from Oliver.'

Neil turned round to face me. 'In what way?'

I pondered. I hadn't liked Sebastian Medway one bit. He was reported to be very clever, and good at just about everything he tried. A shade too good to be true, it seemed to me, and I thought of him as a sanctimonious young prig. Or was I just accepting Oliver's assessment of his stepbrother?

'He's...a more serious type,' I said warily.

'More dependable?'

I shrugged. 'If you like.'

'Do you think,' said Neil, 'that all along it might have been Sir Robert's intention to leave control of the estate to this adopted son, in view of the fact that he thought Oliver was incapable of running it properly?'

I shook my head. 'I can't believe that.'

'Why not? There's no entail involved, is there?'

'No, but the Haslop Hall estate has passed from father to son for at least five generations, so it would be unthinkable for him to will it away from Oliver. That was always Oliver's trump card; he knew that he would triumph in the end.' I sighed. 'Only of course he hasn't now. Oliver and his father were quite fond of each other in a curious sort of way.'

Neil glanced at his wristwatch. 'I seem to remember that they do a good lunch at the Trout Inn. Care to join me?'

I groped for an excuse. 'I haven't finished this list you asked me for.'

'That can wait till this afternoon. You've got to eat.' When I still hesitated, he said, 'Come on, Tracy, I don't bite.'

Me lunching with the detective inspector from Gilchester gave a surprise to the regulars at the Trout. It was obvious that they were speculating about us. Neil grinned, understanding my discomfort.

'You get used to it, Tracy, in this job of mine.'

'I suppose you do.'

'Tell me about *your* job. How do you come to be in that line? You always were artistic, I know.'

'I have my aunt to thank for giving me a push in the right direction,' I said. 'She was a sculptor, you remember.'

Neil grinned. 'She was a formidable lady. Once a crowd of us called round for you to go swimming, and while you were getting ready she showed us her workshop. I was terribly impressed, but scared to open my mouth in case I revealed my abysmal ignorance of things artistic. I had a feeling that she didn't suffer fools gladly.'

'Aunt Verity was an absolute darling, really,' I said. 'It must have been a dreadful bind for her, when my parents were killed and she found herself landed with her little niece. But there was no one else to do it—my mother was an only child. Aunt Verity responded nobly, if somewhat eccentrically. Conventions meant nothing to her, she just went her own way and other people had to like it or lump it.'

The waitress brought the menu. But the choice at the Trout Inn was obvious...trout from the river that bordered its garden. Gently fried in butter, *à la meunière*.

'So,' prompted Neil when she'd gone off with our order, 'your aunt encouraged you.'

'She packed me off to art school in London. And then she urged me to find a job there— even though, as I realised later, her health was failing and she needed me at home. Aunt Verity was a self-sacrificing person, though never in an ostentatious way. She didn't like being thanked.'

'What brought you back eventually?'

'She was dying,' I said simply. 'We both knew there was no hope, even though it wasn't diagnosed as leukaemia immediately. She was furious with me, actually. She called it recklessly squandering my career. But I felt I owed it to her.'

Neil stroked one eyebrow in what seemed to be a characteristic gesture.

'So you stayed and cared for your aunt. But after her death, you didn't want to return to London?'

'I planned to, as a matter of fact. The studio I'd worked for was willing to have me back. But then Sir Robert approached me with the suggestion that I join Oliver in a design business right here in Steeple Haslop.'

Neil looked surprised. 'It was *Sir Robert* who approached you?'

'Yes. The idea was first put into his head by Ralph Ebborn—you know, his agent. Having seen Oliver's flair for interior design, Sir Robert thought that at last this was something he might make a go of. But it was obvious that Oliver would need an assistant with the necessary training.'

'And Ralph Ebborn, how does he tie in with you?'

'His wife had been a friend of my aunt's for years. Grace Ebborn was one of the Murchisons —do you know them?'

'Murchison?' Neil creased his forehead. 'The name's familiar, but...'

'They're an old local family with a pedigree as long as your arm. Not much money these days, but highly respected. After Grace's parents died she was left with just about enough to live on without getting a job, and she involved herself in all kinds of volunteer work...you know, raising money for charity, and being on committees. She must have been nearly forty, and seemed all set for spinsterhood, when to everyone's surprise she married Ralph Ebborn, who'd come to Steeple Haslop just a few months before to be Sir Robert's agent. Actually,' I corrected, 'Ralph came as the *assistant* agent, but his predecessor died of a coronary and Ralph was asked to take over.'

'So Ebborn is not a local man? I'd somehow imagined that he was.'

'Ralph has been here for fifteen years now,' I explained. 'I happen to know that precisely because I was a bridesmaid at their wedding, and I was eleven at the time. Goodness knows why I was asked, except that I was available.

Grace wanted a proper wedding, with lots of confetti and four little bridesmaids in pink, and Murchison relatives were a bit thin on the ground.'

'A very pretty little bridesmaid you must have made, too,' grinned Neil, and let his eyes linger on me.

Our trout arrived, smelling delicious, garnished with tiny buttered new potatoes. My one thin slice of toast for breakfast seemed like a forgotten memory. The waitress asked if we'd like a window open, and from outside, where the lawn had just been cut, drifted the warm scent of new-mown grass. Murder seemed a thousand miles away.

Dissecting his trout, Neil reminded me, 'You were explaining how Ebborn suggested you should be offered a job with Oliver Medway.'

'Oh yes. Well, it was just at the time that Aunt Verity died. She'd left me Honeysuckle Cottage, but I simply didn't see how I could keep it because I had to get back to London to pick up my career again. Then the idea struck the Ebborns that I might be just the person Sir Robert was looking for as Oliver's assistant. I'll always be grateful to them. It meant that I was able to stay on at Honeysuckle Cottage after all. And besides, I welcomed the challenge the job presented.'

'But now,' Neil went on, picking a small bone from his fork, 'everything has collapsed for you. What will you do, Tracy?'

'I don't know,' I said gloomily. 'I shall have to stay on for a while to clear things up, and then...heaven only knows. I haven't been able to think much about the future yet.'

Neil speared a potato. 'Will you go back to London?'

'I expect so.'

'And sell the cottage?'

'I hate the thought of it,' I said with a sigh.

Neil gave me an ego-boosting smile. 'Perhaps you'll find some way of staying on, Tracy. I certainly hope so.'

At least, I told myself, there was something to weigh against the awfulness of the past twenty-four hours. All of a sudden two very personable men both seemed anxious for me to stick around.

So why wasn't I feeling more cheerful?

CHAPTER 4

We had driven to the Trout Inn in Neil's car, and he took it for granted that he'd deliver me back to the Coach House. But I refused, making the glorious afternoon my excuse.

'I need a breath of air, and I shall enjoy the walk.'

'Sure?'

'Quite sure.' I'd had enough of him, suddenly—he and his probing policeman's questions. 'Thanks for the lunch.'

He drove off in the Gilchester direction, while I turned back across the ancient stone bridge that spanned the river, pausing a moment to gaze down at the water glinting in the sunlight, at the pebbles and trailing fronds of greenery, the dark shapes of lurking trout.

As I walked on along the village street, I was conscious of the sleepy hush of a summer afternoon. Bees droned in a lavender hedge; a marmalade cat sat dozing on a mossy wall; and old Mr Pembury, nearly ninety, was nodding contentedly in a basket chair on the porch of his cottage.

Going past the What-Not Shop, I glanced in through the bottle-glass bow window and caught sight of the owner, Ursula Kemp. She spotted me, too, and beckoned.

'Hallo, Tracy!' she greeted me above the jangle of the doorbell. The look on her face was ambiguous, uncertain, as if she felt a smile would be out of place in the circumstances. 'Isn't it dreadful about Oliver? Is there any further news—I mean, about who did it?'

'Not that I know of.'

'I just thought...since you had lunch with that detective inspector...'

The speed of light was as nothing compared with the Steeple Haslop telegraph.

'He'd hardly tell *me* anything, Ursula. I'm still high on his list of suspects.'

'Oh, surely not? What possible reason could the police have for suspecting you?'

She seemed genuinely shocked and upset on my behalf. Ursula was a comparative newcomer to Steeple Haslop. Two years ago, recently widowed, she had chanced upon the village during a holiday in the Cotswolds. She had fallen in love with the place and decided to settle. Opinions were mixed about the likelihood of her making a success of the little shop she had opened, but she seemed to manage. Probably she had some kind of widow's pension, too. Her stock was a shrewd mixture of junk souvenirs for the tourists who passed through the village during the summer months, and some really rather nice pieces. On occasion Oliver and I had made the odd purchase from her.

Well into her forties, Ursula was still an attractive woman. She had a good skin and clear brown eyes, and she wore her silver-streaked hair scooped into a loose coil. Invariably she gave the impression of twin-set neatness which was possibly intended to reassure customers only too used to being ripped-off in such shops. I would have thought that Ursula had enough going for her to find another husband, but she showed no sign of wanting to. The village speculated about her. Had her first marriage been so good she wanted to preserve the memory intact? Or was it a case of once bitten?

'I think the police suspect every person who might conceivably have done it until they are proved innocent,' I told her. 'I suppose that's routine procedure.'

'So that's why they were in here this morning asking questions.'

'What sort of questions?'

'About you, actually,' she admitted. 'I suppose I shouldn't really be telling you this, but it seems only fair to warn you. They wanted to know if I happened to have seen you drive past here yesterday morning before you found Oliver's body.'

So much for Neil's palliness over lunch, I thought furiously.

'What did you tell them, Ursula?'

'I told them the truth—that I *hadn't* seen you. But I don't understand why it should matter so much, Tracy.'

'It's a question of timing,' I said grimly. 'In their minds it's possible that I might have arrived at the Coach House earlier than I said, quarrelled with Oliver, and...and struck him over the head.'

'I see!' Ursula looked at me wide-eyed. 'If only I'd realised! I could have said...well, that I *had* seen you at the time you told them.'

'But you didn't.' Thinking of Tim and the fingerprints, I said, 'It's no good lying to the police, Ursula. They always find out in the end, and it only makes matters worse.'

'Yes...yes, I suppose you're right.' She touched my arm, giving me a comforting little squeeze. 'Don't worry, Tracy, they can't possibly go on suspecting you.' After a brief hesitation, she asked, 'What's going to happen now? Will you try to carry on at the Design Studio without him?'

'I don't see how I can.' A look I couldn't

decipher fleeted across Ursula's face; then I understood. We had recently bought from her a set of cushion covers in hand-blocked linen for a weekend cottage we'd just refurbished for a Bristol wine merchant, and there had also been a pair of carriage lamps. About two hundred pounds' worth altogether. I hastened to add, 'Naturally, I'll be staying on long enough to see that all the accounts are settled.'

'My dear, I wasn't thinking of that,' she protested, flushing.

There was a babble of voices outside. A motor-coach had drawn up by the village hall opposite, and a bevy of women were descending purposefully on the What-Not Shop.

'You've got customers,' I said with the ghost of a smile, and thankfully escaped.

Escape from Ursula, escape from Neil...I walked with a brisk pace through the rest of the village, looking straight ahead of me, determined not to catch another eye. Then on up the hill, with beechwoods on the left and the high stone wall of Haslop Hall on the right. I turned in at the gates and was a hundred yards along the drive when I heard a vehicle coming from behind. I stepped aside to let it go past, but it pulled up alongside me.

'Hallo, Tracy. Want a lift?'

It was Ralph Ebborn, no doubt just returning

from lunch at home. It seemed less trouble to let him drive me the short distance to the Coach House, than to decline his offer and have him linger here for a chat. So I jumped up in the Range Rover beside him.

'I was going to drop in and see you anyway this afternoon,' he said, as he moved off. 'I heard that you were lunching with the detective inspector at the Trout.'

'My God, does *everybody* know that?'

Ralph gave me a sympathetic smile. He was a large man, in his mid-fifties, with a pleasant squarish face. His hair and thick eyebrows were gingery, and he had a rather florid complexion. As usual for work, he wore khaki slacks and a safari jacket, and he carried about his person a vague and not unpleasing aroma of cigar smoke.

'I know how you must be feeling, Tracy.'

'Do you?' I said sarcastically. Then, quickly, 'I'm sorry, Ralph. I didn't mean to take my bad temper out on you.'

He reached across and patted my hand in an avuncular way. 'What did he have to say?'

'Neil Grant, you mean?'

Ralph pulled a face. 'It sounds as if you two made rapid progress over lunch.'

'Oh, but Neil and I have know each other for ages.'

'I see. That accounts for his being so friendly now.'

'I'm not so sure how friendly he is,' I said. 'He has me down on his list of suspects.'

Ralph didn't look shocked as Ursula had done. He just grunted. 'I imagine that it must be a helluva long list. Who else is on it, did he say?'

Tim Baxter, I could have told him. But something checked me. Then, as we swung through the arch into the courtyard, I saw Tim himself getting out of his green estate car. My pulses did a little skip.

'Hallo, Baxter,' Ralph called. 'Is it Tracy you want?'

'That's right.'

I jumped down from the Range Rover and gave Ralph a thank-you salute. But as I went to walk away, he said, 'Hang on a tick. I haven't got around to mentioning what I wanted to see you about. Grace said to invite you for dinner this evening. We'd hate to think of you moping at home all on your own.'

'Thanks, Ralph, I'd like that.' I meant it, too. Grace and Ralph were the two people I'd feel most at ease with just now.

Ralph swung round in a tight circle and drove off. As I turned to unlock the door to the studio, Tim said moodily, 'I needn't have bothered to come.'

I looked at him. 'How d'you mean?'

'I was going to ask if you'd like to eat with *me* this evening.'

'I'm sorry, Tim, but I can't now, can I?'

'There's no need to sound so relieved about it,' he remarked bitterly.

'Don't be stupid.'

I stifled back the uneasy knowledge that I *was* relieved to be provided with a good excuse for refusing Tim. It was crazy...I knew that he wasn't responsible for Oliver's death—he couldn't be—yet the niggle of suspicion refused to go away. Neither of us suggested making it another time. Standing like this at the foot of the stairs, a question darted into my mind. I wondered why I hadn't thought of it before.

'Tim, you never told me why it was you came to the studio yesterday morning.'

He stared at me before answering. 'Does it matter now?'

'It could. I'm surprised that Neil Grant hasn't asked you yet. Or has he?'

'Neil Grant! He's asked me too many bloody questions... He was up at the vineyards this morning, nosing round. Why he wants to nail this murder on me, God knows. But he seems bent on it.'

'Oh Tim, now you really are being stupid,' I protested. 'Neil's just doing his job.'

'Which includes taking you out to lunch? You're very thick with him all of a sudden, aren't you?'

I'd had enough of this. I gave him a furious glare. 'Look, I've got work to do.'

Tim returned my glare for a moment, then, 'Okay, I'll leave you to get on with it.'

Before he'd driven out of the courtyard I realised that he'd not given me an answer about his reason for coming to the studio yesterday. I could still have called him back, but I didn't.

By the time I got upstairs the sound of his car had receded to nothing and everything was quiet. From somewhere far-off on the estate I heard the clatter of a harvester, which only accentuated my feeling of isolation. The sick panic I had experienced this morning came back to me with renewed force. How was I ever going to make myself work in this room?

The sound of the phone crashed through the silence. It was several moments before I could bring myself to pick it up.

'Hullo,' I said huskily.

'Miss Yorke, is that you?' I recognised the voice, hoarse and strained though it was.

'Yes, Sir Robert.'

79

'Ah, good! I tried to reach you at your home.'

'I thought I had better come along to the studio and make a start on sorting things out,' I explained.

'Yes...good...actually, that was what I wished to speak to you about. Er...could you come up to the Hall now, do you think?'

I welcomed any excuse for leaving the studio. And it was a relief, too, to find that sooner than I had expected, Sir Robert was ready to discuss winding up the business. I'd now be able to think about plans for the future.

'Yes, I'll come at once,' I agreed.

Thrusting a notepad and pen into my shoulderbag, I ran downstairs and within two or three minutes I was ringing the bell at Haslop Hall. Grainger let me in and loped ahead of me to Sir Robert's study.

It was a room I had only seen once before when I was first sounded out about joining Oliver. Dark oak panelling rose to head height on all four walls, swallowing the afternoon sunshine. Oliver had not been allowed to change the decor of this sanctum.

Sir Robert was not, as I had anticpated, alone. His adopted son, Sebastian, was seated with him behind the massive leather-topped desk, giving it the appearance of a magistrates' bench. Sir Robert rose politely as I entered, and Sebastian followed suit.

'Please sit down, Miss Yorke,' he invited me, after a little cough to clear his throat. 'Er...you know Sebastian, I believe?'

'Yes, of course.'

Oddly, though there was no blood connection, Sebastian bore a superficial resemblance to Oliver. It struck me that Sir Robert's taste in women had remained consistent as the years advanced...both his previous wives, like the present Lady Medway, had been tall and elegant and raven-haired. But Sebastian lacked his stepbrother's charm. His eyes, dark and long-lashed, were a shade too close together, and there was a tightness to his mouth.

'Sebastian came home from Oxford yesterday to be with us at this dreadful time,' Sir Robert explained, at which Sebastian looked smugly virtuous. The university long vacation had already begun, of course, but I seemed to recall that Oliver had mentioned something about Sebastian staying on for a symposium on international law.

Sir Robert himself looked ghastly, even worse than in those first minutes of shock yesterday. His cheeks and lips were tinged with blue, and I noticed that the hand resting on his desk was trembling.

He cleared his throat again, with some difficulty. 'Oliver's death has, er...placed you in an unfortunate situation, Miss Yorke. I feel to some degree responsible, having persuaded you to abandon your plans to return to London after your aunt's death.'

Sir Robert paused, as if expecting me to comment. But I could think of no comment to make. His next words took me utterly by surprise.

'Would it be possible for you to carry on the Design Studio alone?'

'You mean,' I stammered foolishly, 'run it myself?'

'I would be very ready,' he went on, 'to lend my financial support. As you know, I charged Oliver a purely nominal rent for the premises, merely for bookkeeping purposes, and this arrangement could continue. I could also provide you with the necessary working capital.'

Sebastian's expression was far from approving, but he kept quiet. After some rapid thinking, I said cautiously, 'It's only fair to point out, Sir Robert, that anything I undertook would need to be on a much smaller scale. For one thing, I haven't got Oliver's talent—that was something very special. And for another thing, I lack his contacts. Even if I were able to succeed alone, there wouldn't be much of a return on your investment, I'm afraid.'

'I'm not looking for a profit,' he said tetchily. 'It was your assistance, Miss Yorke, that made it possible for my son to practise a profession which seemed to suit him. I am very much aware of that fact, and this is a way of showing my appreciation.'

It was a marvellous opportunity. So why did I hesitate?

Was it the curious mood that had gripped me earlier this afternoon at the studio, the sense of unease mounting almost to panic? Was it because the horror of Oliver's death was too fresh in my mind? But this would surely pass, as everything has to pass in time.

'You're very generous, Sir Robert,' I made myself say. 'I should be glad to accept your offer.'

'Good!' He gave a satisfied nod. 'Then we shall have a proper agreement drawn up. My solicitor will see to it, Miss Yorke, and be in touch with you.'

That was that; there was nothing more to be said. The matter was settled and Sir Robert wanted the interview over. But the surprising thing was that he had screwed himself up to talk to me at all on this subject, so soon after Oliver's death.

I rose to my feet, and both men stood up too.

'How is Lady Medway today?' I said. The question was asked merely from politeness, but Sir Robert stared at me as if I must have had some other, hidden motive. It was Sebastian who answered.

'My stepmother is indisposed, Miss Yorke, as one might expect after such a shock.' The shock, his tone seemed to imply, resulting from Oliver's lack of consideration in getting himself murdered.

'Yes, of course,' I muttered. 'Naturally. I...I hope she feels better soon.'

Sebastian did not show me out himself, as courtesy might have demanded. Instead, he rang for Grainger, and from the speed with which the butler answered the summons, I suspected that he had been lurking outside the door.

Walking back to the studio I tried to feel elated, but couldn't. Was it because I was gaining from Oliver's death? Or because I lacked sufficient confidence in my own ability? I had a strong feeling that Sir Robert had made his proposition purely from a sense of obligation. And Sebastian clearly opposed the whole idea.

CHAPTER 5

Grace must have been watching for me. Before I had opened the front gate of The Larches she was out of the house and hastening to greet me down on the flower-flanked path. After a hug, she held me back at arms' length to study my face.

'Tracy, you poor girl! How dreadful it must have been for you. I was wondering whether to ring you last evening, but decided that you'd probably had quite enough talking for one day. Come along in, Ralph's seeing to drinks. I expect you could do with one.'

She ushered me up the single step and beneath the pretty fanlight into the long, narrow hall which had been made to appear spacious by the use of gleaming white paintwork and a couple of large mirrors. Ralph appeared in the doorway of the sitting room, a bottle in his hand.

'Hallo, Tracy. Dry sherry okay for you?'

'Thanks.'

He had changed into a dark suit which in Grace's book would be required evening wear at home, even for just the two of them. The comments people often passed about Grace Ebborn behind her back were of the sort that were outwardly kind but carried a mild sting in the tail. *She means well. She likes things to be just so. Her heart's in the right place.* For myself, I found Grace's little faults very forgivable. She was just a shade too house-proud, a bit over-fastidious, and rather strait-laced. If she'd had children, this doubtless would all have been knocked out of her, but she had married Ralph a bit too late in the day for that.

Self-discipline was an important ingredient in Grace's character. Now fifty, she had taken care to keep herself in good shape. Without any pretensions to beauty she always managed to look nice (a word that was frequently on her lips). This evening she had on a moiré silk dress in a soft shade of dark green, with her pearls; and her hair, which she wore in a slightly old-fashioned style, was newly set.

We sat together on the velvet sofa and Ralph handed us our drinks, remaining standing himself before the white-marble fireplace which was filled now with one of Grace's elaborate arrangements of flowers and ferns.

'Well girls, cheers!'

'I had a surprise today,' I said, and told them about Sir Robert's offer.

Grace beamed. 'Oh, that is nice! I'm so glad for you, Tracy. I don't mind admitting that I feel somewhat relieved, too, because it's been rather on our minds—hasn't it, Ralph dear?— that we pushed you into taking that job with Oliver.'

'And it's good to know,' he added, 'that Tracy won't be packing her bags and leaving us.'

He took out his cigar case and received a quick frown from his wife. 'Really, Ralph, not just before dinner! Now, Tracy dear, we haven't asked you here this evening out of morbid curiosity. So if you want to give your mind a rest from the dreadful business of Oliver's death, we'll try to talk about other things.'

I smiled faintly. Yes, Grace always meant well. Yet she herself seemed to accept the impossibility of what she suggested, for her next remark was, 'Ralph tells me that Sir Robert is taking it very badly.'

'Yes,' I agreed. 'It can't have done anything to help his heart condition.'

Grace reached for her glass and took a tiny sip. 'The poor man, he needs all the support he can get at such a time, but I'm sure that he's getting precious little from that wife of his.'

'It must have been a shock for her, too,' I murmured.

'No doubt it was. But it's not the same thing at all, is it? I mean, Oliver wasn't *her* son. Anyway, I doubt if the present Lady Medway possesses much in the way of nice feelings. She has always struck me as being very cold. She makes us feel that it's a real condescension on her part when we're invited to dine at the Hall—which really is the limit when one remembers that she was only an actress, and not a very good one at that, when Sir Robert met her.'

'At least,' I said lightly, 'you *get* invited to dine at the Hall. That's more than I've ever been.'

'Oh, but she *has* to ask us, Tracy. It's a matter of custom for the agent and his wife to be on dining terms with the family. Quite apart from formal dinner parties, Ralph and I are invited alone three times a year. In the previous Lady Medway's day, those evenings used to be a real pleasure for us. But now the atmosphere is far from agreeable.'

I caught Ralph's fond smile of amusement. 'It's all in your imagination, my dear. I've never sensed any particular atmosphere.'

'But then you're a man,' she said impatiently, 'so you wouldn't be aware of nuances. Men are so unobservant.'

'Thank the Lord for that,' he chuckled. 'It

88

makes life a lot less complicated.'

Grace plucked an invisible hair from the skirt of her dress.

'At all events, it was most fortunate that Sebastian was right there on the spot for Sir Robert to turn to when...when it happened. What a blessing that he'd come from Oxford by then.'

'Oh, but Sebastian wasn't already at home,' I said. 'From what Sir Robert said this morning, they must have sent for him.'

Grace drew her eyebrows together in surprise. 'Are you sure, Tracy? I thought...'

'I,' said Ralph, 'am quite sure. Because I was the one who phoned for him to come home. I had quite a job contacting him, too. I tried his college rooms at Oxford, and they gave me another number to try, where there was some kind of legal conference going on. But Sebastian hadn't turned up for it, and no one knew where he was. So I had to leave a message for him to ring me, and I was kept hanging about in the estate office till nearly four o'clock before he finally came through.'

'How strange!' said Grace.

'Why strange?' demanded Ralph. 'I hardly felt that I could go out of the office and leave the job of informing Sebastian that his step-brother had been murdered to one of the clerks.'

'No, that wasn't what I meant.' Grace gave her husband an uncertain glance. 'Sebastian was here in this district yesterday morning. That's why I thought he must be back home.'

Ralph sank down in an armchair facing us and leaned forward. His face was tense.

'What makes you say that Sebastian was in this district?'

'Because I saw him.'

'You saw him!' we exclaimed together, and Ralph added, 'Impossible!'

'But I did! You remember that yesterday morning I drove over to Chipping Nash to make arrangements about having the art exhibition in the library there?'

'What's that got to do with it?'

'I'm telling you, Ralph. When I was returning home I took the back lanes through Nashwick Woods to be quicker, because I was a bit late for preparing our lunch, and even though it was only going to be ham and tongue and a tossed salad...'

'Get on with it,' said Ralph, showing a rare impatience with Grace's love for minutiae.

'Well, I pulled up at the crossroads near Friar's Hollow for another car to go by, and I noticed that the driver was Sebastian Medway. There was someone with him, but I didn't recognise her. He was driving rather fast,

90

considering the narrowness of the lane.'

'What time was this, Grace?' Ralph asked, frowning.

'Just before twelve-thirty. About twenty-five past.'

'What kind of car was it?'

Grace wrinkled her brow. 'You know I'm hopeless when it comes to cars,' she protested. 'It was black...quite big. One of those that have their sidelights on all the time.'

'A Volvo!' he exclaimed. 'Well, there you are then. Sebastian's car at the moment is a Renault. Light blue. So it can't have been him.'

'It was!' she insisted unhappily.

Ralph put down his sherry glass very slowly, as if he was afraid he might spill the wine. He stared between his knees at the dove-grey carpet.

'Which way was the Volvo travelling, Grace?'

'Towards the bridge.'

Ralph took in a ragged breath. I knew what he was thinking, and Grace must have done by now, too. From the Volvo's direction it could have travelled by way of a little used track that skirted the rear of the Coach House and emerged from the park by a farm-style gate not far from the Friar's Hollow crossroads. *Could* have done. There were other possibilities, of course,

91

in such a tangle of small lanes. But anyway, what was Sebastian Medway doing at that spot at that time, when he was supposed to have been in Oxford? If it really was Sebastian...

But I could see from Grace's expression that her conviction was unshaken. And Ralph believed her.

'My God!' he said, after a long moment.

'What are we going to do?' I asked.

'Do?' He gave me a blank stare, and I went on, 'Well, we can't keep this to ourselves, can we? I mean, it may be vital information. The police ought to know.'

Ralph passed a hand slowly across his face. 'Let me think, Tracy. Hang on a bit.'

After the french clock on the mantel had ticked almost a full minute, Ralph said slowly, 'Suppose I have a word with Sebastian about this?'

'What good would that do?' I objected.

'He ought to be given a chance to explain. And if he had a perfectly good reason for being in these parts, instead of at Oxford...well, that'll be that. We'll have avoided dragging the police in and causing a lot of unnecessary unpleasantness for the family.'

'But suppose Sebastian denies being here?' I asked.

'In that case, we'll have to think again.'

I hesitated, then said against my better judgment, 'Well, all right.'

'So you'll leave things in my hands?'

I nodded, consoling myself with the thought that after all, it was much more the Ebborns' concern than mine since Grace was the one who had claimed to have seen Sebastian in the district. All the same, I wondered uneasily what Neil would have to say, if he knew that I had agreed to suppress an important piece of information like this.

Grace and Ralph both made an effort to get back to an easy atmosphere, and I tried my best to respond. Dinner was one of Grace's superb Boeuf Bourguignonnes. But none of us did justice to the excellent food, and too often I found myself turning to the beaujolois with which Ralph kept my glass topped up.

The meal was punctuated by sudden awkward little silences, and I knew that they both shared my own sombre thoughts. Sebastian had been seen in the vicinity of Haslop Hall within minutes of his stepbrother's murder. Sebastian Medway, adopted son of Sir Robert and now his *only* son. The new heir to the Medway fortune.

The church clock was stirring into creaky life for nine o'clock as I slammed the door of Honeysuckle Cottage. I was walking to my garage at the side when I heard the front gate click, and glanced round to see that it was Neil.

'Glad I caught you,' he called.

'Only just! I'm on my way to work.'

He grinned ruefully. 'To tell you the truth, I was hoping to cadge a cup of coffee. I've been on the go since seven this morning, but I didn't much fancy my chance of being served anything drinkable at that scruffy cafe on the Gilchester road.'

I wasn't feeling friendly after his treachery in questioning Ursula about my movements. But I shrugged and turned back.

'Oh, all right. There's nothing so urgent it can't wait for half an hour. What brings you over this way so early?'

'I have an appointment,' he said, and left it at that.

He followed me inside to the kitchen. I filled the electric kettle, and switched on, set out two mugs, and reached for the instant coffee jar. On second thoughts I put it back on the shelf and took down the tin of ground coffee and a filter paper. If Neil rated my coffee, it might as well be good.

He perched himself on the edge of the table and glanced round appreciatively. With the sun streaming in between the orange-check curtains, giving life to the natural pine fitments and rush-matted floor, I wasn't ashamed of my kitchen.

'This is really nice,' he commented. 'But then, considering your profession, I suppose it would be.'

'It's a bit cottagy,' I said, in the way we all have of disparaging our own creations.

'But this *is* a cottage, a genuine old Cotswold cottage. It's not precious, though, that's the important thing.'

'What a surprise,' I laughed, as I poured boiling water on the coffee. 'A detective with an appreciative eye.'

'A very appreciative eye,' he rejoined, and gave me a slow look.

'D'you take sugar and cream?' I asked, turning away.

'Dark brown, please, and two spoonfuls.'

I took mine black, and leant back against the sink unit while I drank it.

Neil spoilt the easier atmosphere between us by asking suddenly, 'Have you seen anything more of Tim Baxter?'

'I have,' I said, in a carefully neutral voice.

He gave his coffee an extra stir. 'When was that?'

'Yesterday afternoon, when I arrived back at the Coach House after lunching with you. He had just called in to see me.'

'Anxious to find out what had transpired, was he?'

'If you mean did Tim know that I'd had lunch with you, the answer is yes. But then so did every single living soul in Steeple Haslop, I imagine, not to mention every cat and dog and budgerigar.'

He grinned. 'But about Baxter...'

'What about him?' My stomach knotted.

'You were going to tell me what he had to say.'

'Was I? Well, Tim asked me to dinner, but I was already engaged.'

'So you made it another day instead.'

'No, we didn't, actually.' I put my mug down on the draining board with a bang. 'If you're looking for a link between Tim and me, you're wasting your time.'

'He rushed to cover up for you concerning those fingerprints,' Neil reminded me. 'Which was a stupid thing to do. Why did he, I wonder?'

'It was just an instinctive response.'

Neil drained the last of his coffee, and held out the mug.

'Any more in the pot?'

'You've got a nerve!' I exploded. 'Coming here expecting me to fill you up with coffee, and all the while making nasty insinuations...'

'People with nothing to hide,' he remarked sententiously, 'have nothing to fear in answering police questions.'

'You think I've got something to hide?'

'Have you?'

He was still holding the mug out, and I took it from him ungraciously, refilling it and adding cream and sugar.

'You'd better hurry up and drink it. I've got to get to work.'

'Have you decided yet what you're going to do?' he asked me. 'Any chance of you staying in this part of the world?'

'I will be, as a matter of fact.' I gave him a brief run-through of my conversation with Sir Robert.

'It's a generous offer,' said Neil. 'Mind you, he'll recover any money he puts up to back you, I've no doubt of that. Still, I wonder why he did it?'

'He feels he owes me something, I suppose.'

'I'm sure he does owe you something—a hell of a lot, I should say. But did the Medways get rich by remembering their obligations?'

'Do I detect a sour note?'

'Probably. My Chief Superintendent has told me in no uncertain terms that I'm to treat the Medway family with kid gloves.'

'Well, they are influential people in this neck

of the woods,' I said.

'In my book the landed gentry are governed by the same laws as everyone else. As it happens my ten o'clock appointment is up at the Hall...with Master Sebastian.'

Damn him, why did he have to bring that name up now? Trying to sound casual, I said, 'Are you seeing him for any special reason?'

'To get some answers. We've made enquiries in Oxford, and he has some explaining to do about his whereabouts on the morning his stepbrother was killed.'

I felt a chasm yawning open. I stammered, 'But...but why were you checking up on Sebastian? What reason do you have for suspecting him?'

'You seem fond of using that word. The young man in question has, by the death of Oliver Medway, instantly become the heir to a large fortune. Don't you think that's sufficient reason for us to make a few enquiries about his whereabouts at the relevant time?'

'I suppose so.'

He gave me a long, thoughtful look. 'You've already made it clear that you don't much care for Sebastian Medway. Would you consider him capable of murder?'

'Why ask me?' I parried.

'Could be that I respect your judgment, Tracy.'

I realised that I had no option but to tell Neil what I knew about Sebastian. Not to do so would be almost as bad as outright lying to the police, and I wasn't prepared to do that—certainly not in order to shield Sebastian Medway. If, as Ralph seemed to expect, he had a perfectly good explanation for his presence so close to the scene of his stepbrother's murder... well, he could give it to the police himself. At least I knew that Neil would be circumspect in the way he set about asking questions. He wasn't going to barge into the drawing room at Haslop Hall and fling out accusations.

So, hesitantly and very unhappily, I told him about Grace having seen Sebastian on Wednesday morning. Neil's expression became grim. As I faltered to a stop he demanded roughly, 'What the devil did you think you were playing at, Tracy, keeping quiet about all this?'

'Well, you see, Ralph wanted to speak to Sebastian first...ask him for an explanation. He said that if he *didn't* get one, then was the time to inform the police. It...it seemed to make sense.'

'It doesn't make any sense at all! Ralph Ebborn can't take it upon himself to judge whether or not this is important. What's his game, I wonder? Trying to protect his lord and master's family?'

'Neil, you can't think that Ralph would deliberately conceal important evidence?'

'He won't get a chance to now, anyway. Before I do anything else, I'm going to have a few words with Ralph Ebborn.' He glanced at the clock on the wall. It was now half past nine. 'Young Sebastian will have to cool his heels until I've finished with Ebborn.'

'Ralph will find it hard to forgive me for telling you,' I said miserably.

'What you ought to be worrying about,' said Neil, 'is whether *I'll* forgive you. You did a damn fool thing, Tracy, and I hope you realise it. I know that it was primarily Mrs Ebborn's responsibility, as the actual witness. But you can't dodge your own responsibility so easily. It was your duty to pass on to the police any knowledge you had which was relevant to the case. And you know it.'

I was reduced to silence. Rising from his perch on the table, Neil reached out his hand and flicked my cheek with his fingertip.

'You make a marvellous cup of coffee.'

CHAPTER 6

To allow time for Neil to get clear, I stayed to rinse out our coffee mugs. While I was drying them, the phone rang.

'Hallo, Tracy,' said Ralph. 'I dropped round to the studio to see you just now. You're late this morning.'

'Yes, I can't seem to get started.'

'I wanted to tell you that I ran into Sebastian first thing this morning. He was out riding, so I took the chance of having a quiet chat.'

'What did he have to say' I asked, my pulse rate suddenly speeding up.

'He was pretty cagey at first. But I pointed out that although I was very reluctant to do so, I would feel compelled to inform the police that my wife had seen him on Wednesday morning —unless he could give me an explanation. So in the end he did.'

'And what *was* his explanation?'

'I'd better not tell you over the phone,' said Ralph. 'Anyway, it doesn't really matter now, does it, as long as we know that Sebastian is in the clear. And I can assure you that he is,

101

Tracy, so we can just forget the whole thing.'

'It's not going to be quite as easy as that, Ralph,' I muttered wretchedly.

'Oh?' he demanded. 'Why not?'

'Because...' But it was no use hesitating; I couldn't avoid admitting what I'd done. So I plunged straight in. 'I've already told Neil Grant about Grace seeing Sebastian.'

'You did *what?*'

'Neil dropped round here just now...that's why I'm late this morning. He was asking me about Sebastian, my opinion of him. Because, you see, they've checked on him in Oxford, and he didn't have a satisfactory alibi for that morning. So...well, in the circumstances I could hardly conceal what I knew, could I?'

There was a pause. Then, 'How did Grant react?'

'He really laid into me for not passing the information to the police immediately. And... and I'm afraid that he's going to do the same with you, Ralph. In fact, he's on his way over right now.'

'God Almighty!' There was another pause, then Ralph muttered, 'I suppose I can always make out that I was planning to phone him about it this morning, and...'

'No, that's no good. Neil knows that you intended to talk to Sebastian, and say nothing if

102

he could give you a satisfactory explanation for being near here on Wednesday morning.'

'You seem to have gone out of your way to put me on the spot,' Ralph said furiously. 'What the hell did you think you were up to?'

'I had to tell him everything, surely you can see that! Not to have admitted it straight out would be tantamount to lying, and that would have made matters a lot worse. I'm sorry, Ralph.'

He started to say something else, but broke off for a moment to speak to someone in the office. 'I gather that Grant has arrived. I'll have to go now.'

Now I was thoroughly in Ralph's bad books, and Grace wouldn't be any too pleased with me, either. Work, I told myself, was the best remedy for depression, and there was plenty to be done! So I took off for the Coach House.

First, I called the carpet firm in Kidderminster and found to my relief that the specially woven broadloom for the Golden Peacock job was being put on rail this morning. A letter had arrived in the morning's mail which promised delivery of the equipment for the Myddleton Manor kitchen next Monday, and I fixed with the contractor about installing it. So far, so good.

Then I turned to something new. Oliver had rough-sketched some ideas for converting an old thatched barn into a pool-side bar and games room, and I tried to concentrate on making a series of coloured visuals for the client's approval. I was getting absorbed at my drawing board, with photos spread out all round me, when the phone rang. As I scooped it up my worries came rushing back in a flood. It would be Ralph to report how he'd got on with Neil.

'Hallo, Tracy, it's Tim. Look, about having a meal with me,' he said, 'how about tonight?'

His call had come at just the right moment. I was beginning to feel like a social outcast.

'Yes, I'd like that, Tim.'

'Great! I'll pick you up...at seven. I thought we might go to the Lamb Inn in Gilchester.' He suddenly sounded diffident. 'Er...how're things going with you?'

'So-so! By the way, I'll be staying on here and running the Design Studio on my own. Sir Robert suggested it.'

'That's wonderful news, Tracy!' His obvious pleasure further boosted my morale.

'I'll tell you all about it this evening,' I said happily, and rang off.

I drove home at lunch-time, collected together a tray-snack of cheese and a chunk of cucumber, crisp bread, an apple, and a glass of milk, and took it into the garden to relax in the shade of the weeping ash tree. The job I'd lined up to do this afternoon I didn't fancy at all, but it had to be faced.

Dodford was a village three miles to the south of Steeple Haslop, enfolded in a specially lovely little valley. The Old Rectory, a largish early-Victorian house, stood adjoining the Norman church opposite the village green.

Cynthia Fairford opened the door to my ring and gave me a startled look. She was one of those women who, though still attractive, live in dread of looming middle-age. Two sons away at boarding school and a prosperous civil-engineer husband who spent half his life dashing off to far-flung regions of the world, left her with too much time on her hands. In a word, she had to be categorised as the perfect target for Oliver's attention.

'Hallo, Mrs Fairford. I thought I ought to come along and see you.'

'Yes,' she said vaguely, pushing back her ash-blonde hair. 'Come in, Miss Yorke.'

She led the way across the hall to her drawing room, for which the Design Studio was planning a face-lift. As I stepped across the threshold it struck me suddenly that Oliver's proposed treatment was quite wrong in here, altogether too gimmicky. This graciously proportioned room, with long windows that opened out onto a canopied verandah and looked across sweeping lawns to a vista of the church tower framed between giant copper beeches, needed something more in keeping with tradition.

Oliver had become much too daring and flamboyant. Suddenly I understood why every now and then the final result had been greeted with less than the whoops of delight that Oliver expected from his clients.

I felt a sneak of disloyalty for doubting Oliver's judgment now, but I also realised that responsibility for work carried out by the Design Studio would be mine alone in the future. So it must reflect *my* ideas.

Cynthia Fairford was, I realised, in a severe state of shock. I trod warily; half afraid that I would precipitate an outburst of grief, half wondering if I should encourage just that, to release some of her pent-up tension. She murmured a few conventional expressions of horror, clearly walking a tight-rope with her emotions. After a few minutes she offered me tea, and was away for twice too long getting it...dragging herself together, no doubt.

Though I could see that she didn't care one way or the other what happened to her drawing room now, she readily agreed to my suggestion of a colour scheme of greens and golds. I had a feeling that it would be therapeutic for her to be forced to take an interest, so I elaborated at some length.

I was about to leave, and we were in the rather splendidly ornate entrance hall with its high lantern dome, before Cynthia's tight self-control showed signs of cracking.

'The police have been here, asking questions,' she said, darting a nervous glance at me.

I said blandly, 'I gather that they're interviewing everybody who had any connection with Oliver.'

Her gaze as it met mine was shadowed with fear. 'He and I..we quarrelled.'

'Oh?' I said slowly. 'Oliver didn't mention it to me. When was this?'

A blackbird singing just outside the window nearly drowned Cynthia's breathy whisper. 'The same morning he was killed, early on. He...he was here, you see.'

Now it was out in the open. But still not to be put into bald, unequivocal words.

'Did you tell the police?' I asked cautiously.

'They knew that he'd been here with me,' she muttered indistinctly. 'That's why they came. I...I didn't tell them that we'd quarrelled, though.'

I thought for a moment, then came to a decision.

'Best to leave it that way,' I said. 'It would do no good for them to know; it would only ...complicate things.' Shaking hands, I pressed her fingers. 'I'm sure you'll hear no more from the police, Mrs Fairford.'

I meant, and she knew I meant, that her husband wouldn't need to hear of the affair. As I drove away, I wondered how Neil had found out that Oliver had spent the night at the Old Rectory. Fred Sparrow...did his milk round extend to Dodford? Had he spotted the red Alfa-Romeo tucked away under the copper beeches early that morning? And had he, taking the pious advice I'd given to his wife, finally volunteered the information to the police?

And here was I, now, daring to advise Cynthia Fairford to conceal relevant information. But I'd be ready to bet my last penny that Cynthia hadn't been the one to kill Oliver.

What could their quarrel have been about? Not the ending of the love affair, it was too new for that. Another woman, most probably. There was always another woman in Oliver's life for his current flame to be jealous of.

When Tim called for me at seven I invited him in for a quick drink. Like Neil, not having seen the inside of Honeysuckle Cottage for years, he made some nice comments on my work. We finished our drinks and I suggested that we get going. But then Tim couldn't find his car keys. He patted his pockets and glanced around in a lost sort of way.

'I'm always doing this,' he acknowledged.

'Is that them on the mantelpiece?'

'Oh yes, good!' He gave me one of his quick, lopsided smiles that I found so endearing.

In his car, as we headed for Gilchester, he said, 'It was great to hear that you'll be staying on in Steeple Haslop, Tracy. You said it was Sir Robert who made the suggestion?'

'Yes, it came as a big surprise. He sent for me, and asked if I'd like to stay on and run the Design Studio. He said I could have the premises virtually rent free, and he's going to provide capital for me to keep going until I'm on my feet. It's very generous of him.'

'Or very shrewd.'

'I suppose I'm meant to take that as a compliment?'

'What else? Sir Robert approves of enterprise, and he can be quite a farsighted old boy, as I have reason to know. He listened to me when I went to him with a crazy idea about starting a vineyard.'

'And now you've proved how right you were?'

'To some extent. But there are still problems.'

'Such as?'

'The dear old British climate, chiefly. Wine grapes *can* be grown successfully in this country. But the quantity and quality is entirely at the mercy of the weather—as wine growers have learnt from bitter experience these past few years. A bad July can ruin not only the current year's vintage, but the following one as well because the new growth suffers. I've been damn lucky myself, and I'm still convinced that wine growing is commercially viable here. But I realise now that a run of bad seasons could bankrupt me. What I'd like to have is a definite understanding that in such an event the Haslop Hall estate would help me ride out the storm. In the long term, it would be a very worthwhile investment for the Medways. I'm absolutely convinced of that.'

'Have you discussed this with Sir Robert?' I asked.

Tim didn't reply at once, seizing the chance to pass a farm tractor that was towing a loaded hay wagon. Then he said, 'It would hardly be fair to expect the old boy to give his attention to business matters right now.'

'No, I suppose not,' I agreed, aware that he hadn't really answered my question.

Tim drove another mile or so before he spoke again. 'Have the police got any theories about the murder yet?'

'I'm not likely to be told if they have.'

'Not even by Neil Grant?'

'Not even by Neil Grant.'

Perhaps it was the result of a conscious effort on both our parts, but as Tim and I entered the Lamb Inn we were in a mood to enjoy a pleasant evening. The food was super, as English as it possibly could be. Steak and mushroom pie, with spinach; strawberries and thick yellow cream; then a ripe Stilton cheese. The surroundings were unostentatiously comfortable. Oliver would have scathingly denounced the Lamb Inn as lacking the faintest spark of originality— food and decor both. But for us, this evening, it was exactly right.

After dinner we sat with our coffee on a balcony overlooking the old coachyard, garlanded with fairy lights and hanging baskets of flowers. From somewhere inside came a soft drift of piano music. Despite the trauma of the past few days I felt happy and excited.

Tim linked his fingers into mine. 'This is good, isn't it? I've been such a workaholic since I started the vineyard that I've managed to forget what it's all about.'

'That's easy to do, I suppose.'

'You won't let it happen to you, Tracy?'

I smiled back at him. 'I'd be a fool to, wouldn't I?'

When we finally reached Honeysuckle Cottage Tim got out of the car and came with me to the gate. His arms went round me, drawing me close, and our lips met in a long, sweet kiss that set all my blood cells dancing with delight.

'Tracy...you're so lovely,' he whispered huskily as he let me go. He wanted to know when we could see each other over the weekend, explaining that unfortunately he and the two men who helped him had scheduled a full working day tomorrow, even though it was Saturday.

'Alas, summer pruning and spraying waits for no one,' he said ruefully.

'If you like,' I offered on an impulse, 'I'll come and lend you a hand.'

'I do like! But I warn you, working among the vines is a bit of a mucky job. Your hands...'

'My hands,' I said, 'are not exactly lily-white. And I'll wear some old jeans.'

He kissed me again, and lingered still longer. We might have been a pair of romantic teenagers. When Tim finally left, my glow lasted while I prepared for bed and drifted off into a happy, untroubled sleep.

I was straightening up the cottage after breakfast when the doorbell rang. My caller was a man I vaguely recognised, but couldn't place...middle height, middle build, middle age.

'Miss Yorke?'

'That's right.'

'I'm Detective Sergeant Willis. Inspector Grant sent me.'

'Oh yes. Come in, won't you?'

Even a man of his modest height had to stoop slightly through my low doorway. I led him into the living room, and gestured to him to sit down. He chose an upright chair.

'What can I do for you, sergeant?'

'I've brought something to show you, Miss Yorke. An anonymous letter. Inspector Grant thought you should see it.'

Something in his tone made me acutely uneasy. I waited for him either to produce the mysterious letter or say something more. He did neither, but just sat there observing me.

In the end, I said, 'Well, hadn't you better show me?'

Unhurriedly, the sergeant reached into his inside pocket and produced an envelope which was unstamped and had just a name on the front. He withdrew the sheet of folded paper it contained and handed it across.

The letter was formed from a paste-up of words and individual letters clipped from a newspaper or magazine, a jumble of different sizes. Wondering, my heart thumping painfully, I read it through.

Whatever she says, Tracy Yorke drove through the village just after half past eleven that day. I ought to know, because I saw her with my own eyes. And if she makes out there was nothing between her and Oliver Medway, that's a laugh. What do you think they got up to when they were alone together in that Coach House place?

The sheet of paper rattled in my shaky fingers, and I could feel sweat on my palms. Glancing up, I found the detective sergeant's gaze fixed on me.

'This...this isn't true,' I stammered. 'It's somebody who...'

He waited in silence, still watching me.

'Who could have sent it?' I asked foolishly. Then, 'How did it come into your hands?'

'Someone dropped it through the letterbox at police HQ during the night. It's addressed to Chief Superintendent Blackley, who is in charge of this enquiry.'

'But surely no one could believe that...?'

'Inspector Grant wanted to have your comments on it, miss.'

114

My eyes flooded with sudden angry tears. 'Why couldn't he bring it himself, instead of sending you?'

'The inspector is a very busy man.' It was said in a reproachful tone.

'I realise that, but something like this...' I faltered to a stop. Was I asking for, expecting, special treatment from Neil Grant because of a long-past friendship when we had been very young?

'It's not a matter of our believing it or not believing it,' said the sergeant, sounding indifferent. 'I'm sure you understand that we have to check on everything, even information given in an anonymous letter. So will you please tell me, Miss Yorke, if there is any truth in what it says. Any truth at all.'

'I've told you already. It *isn't* true, not a single word.'

'What was the exact nature of your relationship with the deceased?'

'There was nothing between us,' I blazed. 'I was his assistant, that's all.'

'What sort of terms were you on with Mr Medway?'

'I've been through all this before, with Inspector Grant.'

'Yes, miss. But I'd like you to answer my questions, if you'd be so kind.'

I bit my lip. 'We were on perfectly normal, friendly terms.'

'Not quite what might be called employer/employee terms?' suggested Sergeant Willis.

'If so, it was because Oliver wasn't that type of man. He was easy-going, casual...'

'Yes, miss?'

'It's in the nature of our sort of work to need a harmonious partnership,' I said. 'We spent a lot of time together, discussing the various projects and sharing ideas. We visited clients' homes together, and...'

The detective sergeant was very good at waiting expectantly. I said, as if I were making a confession, 'All right then, Oliver and I were closer than that usually implies. He took me out in the evening now and again—to have dinner, or maybe to go to the theatre in Cheltenham. Quite often we went riding together for the odd hour, and once or twice this summer we swam in the pool up at the Hall.'

'Mr Medway was a man with...let's say, a considerable reputation where women were concerned. You didn't mind people associating you with him in their minds?'

'Why should I?' I demanded. 'People will think what they want to think. I can't stop them. But there was never anything between Oliver and me. Whoever wrote that anonymous letter is just being spiteful—God knows why. And that person couldn't possibly have seen me drive through the village that morning at eleven-thirty, because I didn't!'

'What was the actual time you came through Steeple Haslop in your car?' he asked.

I was about to protest once again that this was all repetition of my interview with Neil, but I realised that it would cut no ice with this man. He was waiting imperturbably for my answer, his notebook ready, his ball-point poised.

'Between ten-past and a quarter-past twelve,' I said meekly.

After noting that down, the sergeant went on, 'Now I'd like you to recount all your movements that morning, right from the beginning.'

'Very well,' I said, with a sense of defeat. I tried to repeat verbatim what I had told Neil.

'There,' I said when I'd done. 'I hope that satisfies you.'

'Thank you.' He closed his notebook, and stood up to leave.

'But...but what about that letter?' I asked.

'We'll be doing our best to track down the sender, Miss Yorke, you can be sure of that.'

'And if you do?'

'It's a serious offence.' Detective Sergeant

Willis took a step towards the door. 'I'll pass on all you've told me to Inspector Grant. He'll probably be in touch with you again. Good morning.'

When he'd gone I returned to the living room and flopped into a chair, heedless of the passing of time. Goodness knows how much later it was when Tim phoned.

'Tracy! You said you'd be coming over this morning.'

'Yes, I...I was just leaving. Sorry I'm so late.'

'That doesn't matter. Only I was a bit concerned.'

I wouldn't say a word about the letter, I vowed as I drove to the vineyard. Yet when I arrived and Tim came striding between the rows of vines to greet me, I burst out before I could stop myself. 'The police have received a beastly annoymous letter about me, insinuating that I was sleeping with Oliver.'

'I can't understand the mentality of someone like that,' he said slowly, after a moment's silence. 'As if you hadn't enough to put up with.'

'It isn't true,' I insisted.

'Whose business is it, anyhow?' he said with a shrug.

'But don't you understand, Tim, it just isn't true!'

118

Fifty yards off, across the rows of wired vines, a head popped up to see what all the noise was about. One of Tim's two assistants.

'I'm sorry I got hysterical,' I mumbled, feeling foolish.

Tim brushed that aside. 'Did the letter have anything else to say?'

'It virtually accused me of murdering Oliver. Whoever wrote it claimed to have seen me driving through the village that morning a lot earlier than I actually did.'

'Oh?' He gave me a worried look. 'Are the police taking it seriously?'

'They take everything seriously. Neil Grant sent a sergeant to interview me this morning, and I had to go through my movements up to the time I found Oliver's body all over again—every last detail. They're trying to catch me out in a discrepancy, I suppose.'

'It'll blow over, Tracy,' he said soothingly, and went to put his arms round me. But I stepped away. I didn't want to be comforted by Tim at the moment. Despite my denial, I felt sure that he still believed I had been one of Oliver's many bedmates.

At first it seemed light, easy work to move slowly along a row of vines and nip out all the soft sideshoots that were sapping the plants' energy. But after a time, with the sun beating down on my back, I began to feel enervated. I experienced odd hallucinations about finding myself arrested and charged with murder, and nobody to come to my rescue.

When at twelve forty-five I announced abruptly that I was going home, Tim protested, 'But I thought you'd be having lunch here with me.'

'No, I must get back. I...I have things to do.'

'Okay, if you say so. About this evening, though—what time shall I...?'

'I don't think I can see you this evening, Tim.'

I went to turn away, but he caught my arm. There was harshness in his grip, and harshness in his voice.

'Tracy, don't take it out on *me!*'

I stared back at him, blinking, cursing the stupid tears that made my eyes swim. Tim bent his head and dropped a light kiss on my brow.

'If you must go, then go. I'll be round for you at seven.' There was no question, just a simple statement. And I didn't argue.

CHAPTER 7

From the vineyard to Honeysuckle Cottage, the short cut lay through the grounds of Haslop Hall. Lady Medway was cantering across the turf on her chestnut mare, elegantly turned out in white breeches and black velvet jacket. To my surprise she flagged me down with her riding crop. I braked and slipped into neutral as she drew alongside.

'Hallo, Tracy. What are you doing here on a Saturday?' Her friendly manner was astonishing. 'You've been clearing up at the studio, I suppose. I don't blame you for being in a hurry.'

'I'm sorry, Lady Medway?'

'I honestly don't know how you can set foot inside that place at all,' she continued. 'It would seem spooky to me. I expect you can't wait to turn your back on Steeple Haslop once and for all.'

I stared at her, puzzled and a bit embarrassed. 'But I'm staying on, didn't you know? Your husband suggested that I should. He said that if I wanted to keep the studio going, he would help me out financially.' Was I putting my foot in it, I wondered? But in the name of goodness why didn't Lady Medway know? 'It's extremely kind of Sir Robert,' I added. 'I really appreciate it.'

Diana Medway had paled; deeply mortified, it was clear, at being made to look a fool. Unable to pretend that she'd known all along about her husband's offer, she said with an expression of understanding pity. 'Poor dear Robert! All this upset has made him dreadfully forgetful. But I'm so glad for you, Tracy. Er...what about the flat, you're not having that too, are you?'

'Oh no. I daresay some kind of alterations will be done, and the flat let to someone. Unless Sebastian wants it, of course.'

The very mention of Sebastian's name brought forth a downcurving of Lady Medway's lips. It wasn't surprising that Sir Robert's third wife and the adopted son of his second marriage had small liking for one another. And having in mind Sebastian's toadying character —as Oliver had described it to me—I could well imagine that there would be quite a bit of jockeying for position between the two of them.

The chestnut mare was getting restive, perhaps disliking the sound of the car engine. But Diana Medway kept her standing there with a tight grip on the reins.

'Since you're staying on, Tracy, I hope that you'll continue to ride sometimes. I'm concerned that the other horses won't be getting enough exercise now that Oliver isn't here.'

'In that case,' I replied, an idea zooming into my mind, 'perhaps I could bring a friend, Lady Medway?'

She looked far from overjoyed. 'As long as it's someone who knows how to ride properly and won't do a horse more harm than good.'

'I wouldn't invite anyone who wasn't perfectly competent,' I said in a cool voice.

'Oh well, in that case...' She jerked the bridle impatiently to control her mare. 'Are the police still bothering you?'

I certainly wasn't going to mention that anonymous letter and give her the chance of gloating at my expense.

'I'm still not done with them yet,' I said, forcing a light, rueful smile. 'But I imagine none of us are.'

Her lovely violet-blue eyes flickered. 'Why do you say that?'

'I presume they'll go on asking questions until they finally get at the truth.' I slipped the car into gear, and said as I started to move. 'Thanks for the offer of some riding. I'll take you up on it.'

Driving on, I went via the stables to have a word with Billy Moon. I found the old chap in the tack room, intent on the job of cleaning leather saddlery. He was a small, wiry man, and looked as if he might have been a jockey once upon a time. A widower now, with a cottage down by the old estate laundry, he made his work with the horses his entire life.

'Good day to you, Miss Yorke.'

'Hallo, Billy. I see you're busy as usual, even on Saturday. Don't you ever take any time off?'

'I got far too much to do for skivvin', miss, if them horses are to be looked after proper.'

Billy took great pride in his work and kept his charges immaculately groomed; their stalls clean, their saddlery supple and polished. I realised how it must have cut him to the quick to be the victim of Oliver's heavy sarcasm. A thought darted into my mind—but it was crazy and I thrust the idea away. Still, I was left with a silly niggle of doubt about whether it was my conscientious duty to inform Neil Grant that the old man had a reason for hating Oliver Medway.

'I came to ask if I could use a couple of the horses this evening,' I said. 'It's with Lady Medway's permission. She told me she wanted them ridden, you see.'

Billy nodded, and asked, 'Who else will it

be for, Miss Yorke? I mean, you'll be riding Ella same as usual, and if it's another lady she'd better have Silver Socks. But a gent would find Prince more to his liking.'

'Well, I haven't actually asked him yet, but it was Tim Baxter I had in mind.'

The weathered old face darkened. 'That there vineyard chap? You want to be careful of getting yourself mixed up with the likes of him.'

'Why ever should you say that, Billy?' I was genuinely astonished. I couldn't imagine any way in which Tim could have upset him. Their paths hardly ever crossed.

The old man's expression became stubborn, and I knew that I'd get no answer. So instead of pressing the matter, I said, 'By the way, you'll still be seeing me around here. I'm going to stay and run the Design Studio on my own.'

Billy made no comment on that beyond a grunt. 'What time shall I have them horses saddled and ready for you?'

'I don't want to put you to any trouble,' I said. 'I was just checking that it would be okay to take them out this evening. Tim and I can saddle them up for ourselves, and see to them afterwards.'

'No, miss. You just tell me what time.'

'Well...seven o'clock, then,' I said helplessly, resolved to buy him some tobacco as a small present.

I slipped upstairs to the studio to phone Tim. He'd still be working among the vines, I knew, but there was an external bell fitted. I listened to a dozen rings before he answered.

'Tim, this is Tracy. About this evening...'

'I thought I'd made it clear,' he interrupted, 'that I'm coming round for you at seven.'

'How would you fancy a ride?' I explained about meeting up with Lady Medway. 'You used to be quite keen, I seem to remember.'

'Sounds like a good idea. It would be nice to get back in the saddle again after so long.'

'So I'll see you in the stableyard at seven. Suitably attired.'

'Right.'

Mood is a peculiar thing. Nothing had really changed, yet suddenly I felt happy again. I slipped down the stairs into the afternoon sunshine, called goodbye to Billy, and drove off home for a lunch of bread and cheese.

Only there wasn't any cheese left, I found. I'd neglected my shopping these past few days and would need to replenish the larder before the village store shut for the weekend.

The beech trees in the park cast long shadows

as Tim and I set off towards the home farm gates. My mount, the pretty roan mare Ella, and Prince, the grey stallion, were well accustomed to being ridden together. But to me it seemed strange that my companion was not Oliver. His death was driven home to me in a new way.

Tim and I knew one another's early backgrounds, and we discussed mutual friends. Then the conversation turned to the vineyard.

'It sounds to me like unremitting hard work,' I observed.

'You're not far wrong. It's backbreaking a lot of the time, and heartbreaking the rest. You must wonder why the hell I do it.'

'No, I think I understand. The great thing is that you're your own boss. Actually, if I weren't caught up in the design business, I can imagine working on the land, in one form or another.'

He gave a dry laugh. 'You ought to try pruning a few hundred vines on an icy January day, crouched on your haunches with the east wind freezing your fingers. You feel like cursing the bloody Romans for ever introducing the vine to Britain.'

'There must be good times, though, to compensate.'

He glanced at me, and I saw that his eyes were alight.

'Come the vintage, Tracy, that's really great. When you've had a good year, I mean, which isn't all that often. There's nothing like it on a soft October day with the smell of ripe fruit in the air. I get a dozen chaps and girls from round here to help with the picking...the way I find it works best is to put one of each sex on either side of a row. It increases the output no end! And at lunch-time we all repair to one of the winery sheds where Mavis Price and Joan Easton have laid up a terrific spread, and big jugs of last year's wine. Everyone gets a bit tipsy, and the afternoon is rather less productive than the morning.'

We had long since left the Haslop Hall grounds behind and were wending our way along a bridle path beside the river. The sun, slanting through the willow trees, glinted on the water.

'How much wine do you reckon to produce?' I asked Tim. 'I've just no idea of the sort of scale involved.'

'In our best year we picked about thirty-five tons of grapes, which yielded well over thirty thousand bottles.'

'That sounds an *enormous* amount.'

'It's pretty good for the acreage involved,

which of course is tiny by continental standards. I wish we could equal it every year.' Tim sighed. 'Anyone who starts a vineyard in England has to be a bit of a lunatic.'

I laughed.

We jingled on in a companionable silence, emerging onto a lane a quarter of a mile from Haslop St John. At the Barlow Mow we decided to stop for a drink. There was a rustic bench facing the triangular village green, and I tethered the two horses while Tim went inside to fetch us two half pints.

'When I walked into the bar,' he told me when he emerged, 'the conversation stopped dead.'

I smiled ruefully. 'I bet they're talking all the harder now.'

Billy Moon was waiting for us when we got back, sitting in the violet-shadowed yard smoking his pipe. He was grateful for the tobacco I had given him, but Tim he couldn't even bring himself to acknowledge. It distressed me, but Tim seemed not to notice anything.

We drove back to Honeysuckle Cottage each in our own car. I'd bought some sliced ham this afternoon, and I made a big salad to go with it. Tim had brought along a bottle of his own wine.

'I'm afraid it's got somewhat tepid in the

car,' he said, 'so we'll commit the unpardon-able and stick it in the ice compartment of the fridge for ten minutes.'

The atmosphere over the meal was cheerful and relaxed, but our eyes kept meeting across the table and I could sense the tension building up between us. I made some coffee but we never got around to drinking it. As I set down the tray Tim put his hands on my shoulders and turned me round to face him. The next moment we were clinging together in a passion-ate kiss. It was very late when Tim left.

Sunday morning could have been lie-in time, but I was up early. Happiness, too, can make you restless, I pottered around, doing nothing in particular. I was still drinking breakfast coffee when the phone rang.

'Hallo, Tracy. This is Neil. I was just check-ing to know if you'd be in. I'd like to drop by and see you.'

'On a Sunday?' I objected.

'You don't imagine that makes any difference in a murder investigation, do you? I wish to God it did, I could do with a day off.'

'You could always delegate someone else to do your dirty work,' I pointed out coldly. 'It wouldn't be the first time.'

'As a matter of fact, sending Detective

Sergeant Willis to see you did produce an interesting result.'

'And what was that?'

'The story you told him, and the story you told me, didn't tally in every particular.'

'But they must have done,' I protested. 'I told the truth to both of you.'

'You told *me* that you took your watch to the repairers' in Cheltenham on Wednesday morning. But you made no mention of that to the sergeant.'

'Oh...I must have forgotten!' Quite suddenly rage took hold of me. 'You mean you've noted that down as a black mark against me, a simple little oversight? That sort of thing could happen to anyone if they were asked for every tiny detail of their movements days after the event...'

'Have you finished?' enquired Neil calmly. 'If you'd allow me to get a word in edgeways, I could tell you that if anything it's a small point in your favour. We know you did go to the repairers' when you said you did...checking up on that was a routine matter. But there's such a thing as being too word perfect, and that's when we get suspicious.'

Feeling slightly deflated, but still angry, I muttered, 'Have you got any clue about who sent you that letter?'

'Not yet, but we're working on it. I can be with you in about half an hour. Okay?'

'If you must.'

He had robbed the day of its brightness. I wished that I'd been out when he phoned, but it was too late now. I waited for him nervously.

The moment Neil walked in the door, he tossed at me, 'Are you being wise, Tracy, seeing so much of Baxter?'

It was done deliberately, of course, to throw me. And he succeeded.

'Is it the slightest business of yours?' I demanded angrily.

'In the sense, can I prevent you...no. But it's not helping me one bit.'

'I'm so sorry.'

Neil gave me a really dark look. 'You're muddying waters that are murky enough already. Having dinner at the Lamb on Friday evening, up at his place yesterday morning, and out riding with him in the evening.'

'You must have spies everywhere.'

'And a good job, too,' he retorted. 'If we relied solely on volunteered information, we wouldn't get far in this village.'

'Have you got someone tailing me round the clock, or something?'

'My information about you is purely accidental. You being at the Lamb...well, that's almost on the doorstep of police headquarters, so it's hardly surprising that you were seen. Then one of Baxter's workers had a lunch-time drink in the bar of the Trout Inn yesterday, and he happened to mention that you'd spent the morning helping out at the vineyard...the locals have got to find something to chat about while they drink their ale. And as for the riding, the two of you were seen arriving at the pub in Haslop St John on horseback. My men are careful to report everything that could have the smallest relevance.'

Feeling cornered, I resorted to sarcasm. 'And what other terribly vital information have your spies brought back? I stocked up with groceries at the village store yesterday afternoon, did you get that? Perhaps the police concluded that I'm preparing for a siege.'

'You'd be surprised what can be picked up in a village pub,' Neil said equably. 'Would I have discovered in any other way that Sir Robert and Lady Medway had the very dickens of a quarrel on Wednesday morning?'

'Oh? What about?'

'Regrettably, the details weren't forthcoming. Are they in the habit of quarrelling?'

'I'm not on close enough terms with them to know about that.'

'But you sounded very surprised. Did Oliver

133

Medway ever discuss his father and stepmother with you?'

'Not what you'd call discuss, just the odd comment about them from time to time.'

'What sort of things did he have to say?'

I shrugged. 'He was a bit tickled at the idea of his father taking a wife more than twenty years younger than himself. He used to make rather coarse jokes about it.'

'But I never heard anything to suggest that she and Sir Robert didn't get along reasonably well. I suppose that explains the curious atmosphere between them after the news of Oliver's death.'

'Atmosphere?'

'They seemed so cold and distant with each other. Not at all as you'd expect a husband and wife to be after hearing such dreadful news. And it doesn't look,' I continued, 'as if their quarrel has been made up, either, because Sir Robert hadn't said anything to her about my staying on at the Design Studio. It was clearly news to Lady Medway when I mentioned it to her yesterday.'

'Perhaps,' suggested Neil, 'he's the sort of old-fashioned husband who doesn't like to discuss business affairs with his wife?'

'No, I wouldn't have thought Sir Robert was like that. And besides, Lady Medway was obviously livid at not knowing.'

After a brief pause, Neil asked, 'How did Lady Medway get on with Oliver?'

'So-so. He used to consider it a huge joke the way his stepmother puts on air and tries to queen it with the locals. But I doubt if he actually said anything to her face. I don't really know what Lady Medway thought of him. She was very pleased, though, with the way Oliver redesigned her boudoir and some other rooms at the Hall when she first came here.'

'And her other stepson, Sebastian? What was their relationship like?'

'According to Oliver, they don't like each other much. It's understandable, I suppose. Sir Robert taking a third wife can't have pleased Sebastian. He probably lives in fear that she will bear Sir Robert other children. And another son—or a daughter, come to that—in the bloodline, might jeopardize his position somewhat.'

'Could be.'

I asked, 'How did you come to learn about Sir Robert and Lady Medway having quarrelled that morning? I mean, who was talking about it in the pub?'

'I'm sorry, Tracy, but I'm not prepared to tell you that.'

'In which case,' I said frostily, 'aren't you

taking a big risk in disclosing even this much information to me?'

'Why?' He threw me a very stern look. 'Do you intend to pass it on to someone else?'

I flushed, knowing that he meant Tim.

'There are one or two other bits and pieces we've come across that you might be able to comment on,' Neil continued. 'For instance, that the stable-hand at Haslop Hall had no great liking for Oliver Medway.'

'Oliver was a bit withering with him sometimes, that's all. Billy Moon is an inoffensive old man who never harmed anyone.' Even as I spoke I knew that I'd reacted too swiftly in Billy's defence, so I added as a counterweight, 'He's an odd-ball character, and he's apt to take sudden dislikes to people.'

'Oh? Who else, for example?'

I lifted my shoulders to show how totally without significance it was. 'Well, for some weird reason he seems anti-Tim Baxter at the moment.'

'Why's that?'

'Goodness knows! I can't imagine Tim ever having done anything to upset him.'

Neil didn't pursue that, to my relief. Instead, he said, 'About the owner of the What-Not Shop...Mrs Ursula Kemp. What was Oliver Medway's attitude towards her?'

'He liked her, and they seemed to get on well together. Now and again we used to buy things from her shop.'

'Like the fertility god statuette? Did that come from her, by any chance?'

'It did, as a matter of fact.'

'It's rather unlikely, wouldn't you say, that Mrs Kemp would have purchased such an object to put on display in her shop window? More likely she saw it at a sale somewhere and bought it because it was just the sort of thing to amuse her friend Oliver Medway.'

He was dead right. I said, 'So what?'

'It suggests that they were on close terms. Very close terms, perhaps.'

'Oh, come off it! Ursula must be nearly fifteen years older than Oliver was.'

'Would that have prevented her from hoping? She's an attractive, well-preserved widow. Oliver Medway, by all accounts, was the kind of man that women pursue. Did Ursula Kemp pursue him, d'you imagine?'

'No, I can't buy that,' I said emphatically. 'And as for Oliver, he found her amusing company.'

'So he'd drop in there quite often...to look over her stock and enjoy a bit of chit-chat?'

'But that's all it ever was,' I said. 'I'm quite positive. You're not seriously suggesting that

Ursula might have killed him?'

'I'm suggesting nothing. At present she rates no higher as a suspect than a number of other people.'

'Including me?'

Neil was unperturbed. 'We always have to look for motive, Tracy, as well as opportunity. Now what would your motive have been—assuming it's true, as you so vehemently insist, that there was no 'relationship' between you and Oliver.'

'I *had* no motive. I didn't kill him.'

'On the other hand,' he suggested, 'if you two had been having an affair...'

'But we weren't!' I said shrilly. 'Why won't you believe that?'

'If only I could, Tracy, without the tiny reservation I'm obliged to keep in the corner of my mind.'

Why wouldn't he go away and leave me alone, I thought desperately. But first there was something I wanted to know from him.

'What was the outcome of your interview with Ralph Ebborn?' I asked. 'I haven't heard from Ralph since.'

'I'm not surprised that he's keeping a low profile,' Neil commented. 'He was a thoroughly chastened man when I'd finished with him.'

'And Sebastian Medway?'

'What about Sebastian Medway?'

'You said he had some explaining to do,' I reminded him.

'Which he has now done.'

'So Sebastian *is* in the clear, just as Ralph said? All the big fuss you made was over nothing.'

'I didn't say that he was in the clear,' Neil pointed out. 'I merely said that he has given me an explanation for his presence in this area on Wednesday morning. It's been checked on and—as far as it goes—it holds water. But it doesn't mean that he couldn't also have killed his stepbrother.'

'Then Sebastian is still a suspect?'

Neil smiled grimly. 'You see what I mean about murky waters, Tracy?'

He had the nerve to suggest that I provide him with coffee once again. And I was weak enough to agree—though I was anxious to see the back of him. Tim and I had planned to go out for the day, taking a picnic lunch, and I'd got things to do before he arrived.

I hurried with the coffee, and as we were finishing it, Neil said, 'Do you take the magazine *Cotswold Illustrated?*'

I nodded. 'As a regular advertiser, the Design Studio gets sent a voucher copy each month.'

'Then, if you don't mind, I'd like to glance at the June issue.'

'But I haven't got it here, Neil. It's at the studio.'

'I see. Could we go over there now, do you think?'

'What, now?'

'It's rather important,' he said. 'It won't take long.'

I glanced surreptitiously at the kitchen clock. Tim was due in twenty minutes.

'All right, then,' I agreed grudgingly.

Outside, it was obvious that Neil expected to drive me to the Coach House. But I didn't want that, because then he would have to bring me back again and there'd be the danger that he and Tim would meet at the front gate.

'I'll take my own car and follow you,' I said, and ad-libbed when Neil looked at me questioningly, 'I might decide to stay on at the studio and do a bit of work.'

To my relief, Neil didn't hang about at the studio. When I'd found the copy of the magazine he wanted, he riffled through the pages quickly and handed it back to me with a smile.

'Okay, Tracy, that's fine. I'll be seeing you.'

CHAPTER 8

The Coroner's Court, a small, square room in Gilchester's municipal offices, was jam packed. Naturally enough, the violent death of a member of a prominent local family had aroused great interest. Yet the proceedings themselves held no surprises. After a few desultory questions put to the witnesses, Tim and myself, the pathologist, and a police representative, the verdict was murder by person or persons unknown.

In that stuffy, overcrowded little courtroom, I sat beside Tim and watched the faces around me. Sir Robert Medway, looking desperately ill...and Lady Medway. Though seated next to her husband, she seemed distant from him in spirit. Was it because their quarrel had been so bitter they'd still not made it up? Or were they both frozen in mutual fear of something that threatened them equally? Did the clue lie in Sebastian, sitting on the other side of his adoptive father, looking thoroughly frightened? Were Sir Robert and Lady Medway aware that the police had been questioning

Sebastian and had reservations about his alibi? Could it be that they knew for certain something that the police were only guessing at?

I swivelled my eyes along the rows. Apart from the Ebborns, the estate staff had kept away—out of deference to Sir Robert's feelings, no doubt. Grace and Ralph had acknowledged me coolly as we came in. I wished I could justify myself by pointing out that Ralph was wrong in believing that Sebastian's explanation —whatever it was—had completely cleared him of all suspicion. But that, I felt, would be a breach of Neil's confidence, so I could only hope that time would heal the rift between us.

Near the back of the courtroom I picked out Ursula Kemp. She sat bolt upright on the bench, tense, alert to every word that was said. When the murder weapon was produced, she closed her eyes and even at this distance I saw her shudder. The little joke between her and Oliver had tragically misfired.

The coroner wound up by expressing his sympathy with the bereaved family, and it was all over. There was uncertainty and much shuffling about the order of departure. When we were outside on the steps, Tim said, 'Do I see you this evening, Tracy?'

'I...I'm not sure.'

Our outing yesterday hadn't been a success.

Quite why I didn't know. But somehow the session with Neil had depressed me and I was left feeling uneasy. Around tea-time I'd suggested calling it a day. I'd wheeled out the hoary old headache excuse, and Tim had pretended to believe it.

He seemed to understand that my mood was still fragile.

'I'll ring you later on, then,' he said, 'and we'll see how you feel.'

Our attention was caught by the sound of a fiercely revving engine. A small green car was being jerkily manoeuvred from the mass of vehicles parked on the cobbled forecourt. As we watched, its offside front wing narrowly missed scraping the paintwork of a gleaming new Rover. The driver was Ursula Kemp.

'The woman must be crazy,' Tim muttered.

It had struck me, watching Ursula in the courtroom, that Oliver's friendship must have meant a great deal to her. She didn't seem to have many friends. I still felt convinced that Oliver had never been her lover—and that Ursula had never wanted him to be—but that didn't mean she mightn't have been deeply fond of him.

At last Ursula got her car disentangled. With an ill-judged swerve, she turned out into the flow of traffic.

'I can't imagine why she came here this morning,' Tim remarked, as she drove off along the main road. 'It's just sheer bloody morbid curiosity.'

'She and Oliver were very good friends,' I remonstrated.

'For God's sake! Medway would never have been interested in a woman her age.'

'You're like everyone else,' I said bitterly. 'You automatically assume that if Oliver was friendly with a woman, there had to be sex between them.' I threw him a dangerous, challenging look.

Tim didn't meet my eyes. With a glance at his wristwatch, he said, 'I must get back...I'm in the middle of spraying. Having to come here has taken a big chunk out of my day. I'll be in touch when you're in a better mood.'

As I watched his lanky figure striding off I regretted my snappiness. I was of two minds whether to call him back and apologise.

A voice behind me, sounding rather pleased, remarked, 'You two had a tiff?'

I greeted him without enthusiasm.

'I'm glad I caught you before you left, Tracy. I wanted a chat.'

'You're always wanting a chat!'

Neil's grin was unamused. 'How about a drink? Like me, I expect you could do with one after that courtroom.'

'I've got to get home,' I said. 'Anyway, I'm driving.'

'Just one drink. I've got something to tell you.'

Curiosity won, and we walked together to a nearby pub, the Coach and Horses.

The lounge bar, ceilinged with oak beams and furnished with high-backed benches, was very crowded. Not at all the place for a confidential conversation. So Neil and I carried our drinks outside to the pub's garden which backed onto the canal. Two swans were gliding by, and across the water an old man was fishing from some steps. We sat down on a bench beside a buddleia bush that was alive with tortoise-shell butterflies.

Neil took a long swig of his beer, then set the tankard down on a sawn-off tree stump. 'About that anonymous letter, Tracy.'

'You mean you've discovered who sent it?'

He shook his head. 'Not yet. But we *have* discovered an interesting fact. All the words and letters that were used to make up the message had been clipped from the same magazine—last month's issue of *Cotswold Illustrated*.

I stared at him in bewilderment. 'For pity's sake, if you were checking to see if my own copy had been cut up...that's crazy! I'd hardly send the police an accusing letter about myself.'

'From our standpoint, that's too simplistic a view of human nature,' said Neil with a sigh. 'People have been known to do the strangest things. Besides, someone else might have got hold of your copy, so we had to check. Mind you, we don't actually expect to find the cut-about copy. The sender of that letter is unlikely to have left the evidence lying around for anyone to find.'

'How do you know which particular magazine was used?' I asked him. 'And how can you be sure that all the clippings came from the same issue?'

Neil looked a bit smug. 'We observed that the clipped-out pieces were all on art paper, the sort used for the glossy monthlies. Furthermore, the type faces, whether large or small, roman or italic, were confined to just two styles.

'I suppose by "we", you really mean yourself,' I commented, a trifle acidly.

'It was, I admit, used rather in the royal sense. So then we got the laboratory to lift the clippings off the sheet of paper they'd been stuck to, so as to see what printing was on the reverse side of them, On one of the larger pieces, there was a little silhouette logo of a man reading a book, and it struck us...'

'You, again?'

'It struck *me* that this is used regularly to head the book page in *Cotswold Illustrated*. I sent out for a copy, which confirmed this. But nothing in the current issue seemed to match up with the printing on the cuttings, front *and* back. Then it further struck me that probably a back number of the magazine had been used. A young detective-constable was forthwith dispatched to the public library, and lo and behold ...every single clipping could be matched on both sides in last month's issue.'

'So what did you do next—that is, apart from coming to look at my copy?'

'Next we asked the publishers of *Cotswold Illustrated*, a firm in Gloucester, for a list of postal subscribers and advertisers in the Steeple Haslop area—we had to dig someone out on Saturday afternoon to do that. And in addition, we asked the village store for the names of those customers who have a regular order. As you might expect, the two lists together produced a fairly up-market collection of people. We then set about making discreet enquiries.'

'And what emerged?'

'Nothing conclusive, I'm afraid. But then, we hardly expected that. Of those within the inner circle of the murder case, so to speak, we had the following. First, Haslop Hall—an annual postal subscription. When the magazine arrives each month, it is placed on a table in the library and the previous issue removed. The manservant there...what's his name?'

'Grainger.'

'Yes, Grainger. He was a little coy about it, but eventually admitted that he sends the magazine to his daughter in Canada each month, to keep her in touch with home.'

'So that copy is ruled out as a possible?'

'No, that's the odd thing. Apparently the previous issue wasn't there when Grainger went to make the usual switch the other day, and he didn't like to make a point of asking the family about it. He grumbled that he would have to fork out his own money for another copy, when he next goes into Gilchester, because he knows that his daughter is following a series of articles they're running on Cotswold villages.'

'So that means...' I burst out eagerly. But before I could say another word, Neil cut across me, his tone severe.

'It means this, no more and no less...*just possibly* the Haslop Hall copy was the one used to compose the anonymous letter. Beyond that, there's nothing to go on.'

'Are you saying that all this investigating of

yours hasn't really helped at all?'

'Tracy,' he reproached me, 'you insist on expecting everything to be solved in one great blinding flash.'

'The jigsaw puzzle,' I muttered, reminding myself.

'Precisely.'

'So who else takes the magazine?' I asked. 'Or aren't you going to tell me?'

'Why not? There's Tim Baxter.'

'Oh no, you're not still after him!'

'Baxter,' persisted Neil, 'advertises regularly in *Cotswold Illustrated*, like yourself. When he receives his voucher copy each month, he glances at anything that interests him, cuts out his advertisement for the file, and throws the rest away. That's his story, anyway.'

'Don't you believe it?' I demanded furiously.

Neil ignored that. 'I thought the Ebborns worth checking on—they were on the list. But when one of our chaps called there yesterday, Mrs Ebborn was able to produce last month's copy instantly. She knew exactly which cupboard to go to.'

'I can imagine. Grace is always very efficient.'

'Is she? Not so Mrs Fairford, anyway. Apparently she was in a real dither and almost had to ransack the entire house before she tracked down her copy. But she did, eventually, and it was in pristine condition. I feel rather sorry for that woman, being stuck there alone in that house with her husband somewhere in South America, and both her sons away too. She's let this whole business prey on her mind.' He glanced at me questioningly. 'I presume you know about the affair between her and Medway?'

I nodded, and said thoughtfully, 'I'm quite certain that the only reason Cynthia Fairford ever succumbed to Oliver was because she was desperately lonely. If you want my opinion, Neil, she was quite madly in love with Oliver.'

'That's my impression, too.' He picked up his tankard of beer and held it against the light. 'I'd say that her present state of nerves isn't caused by guilt, but by grief.'

'Heavens above!' I exclaimed. 'Did I hear that correctly? Detective Inspector Neil Grant actually basing his judgment on something other than cold, hard, provable fact.'

'Isn't it lucky for some people,' he said, switching his gaze to me, 'that once in a while I do?'

I asked hastily, 'Do you have anyone else of interest on your list?'

'Yes. Mrs Ursula Kemp. Now there's a strange woman.'

'Strange?'

'Didn't you spot her in court this morning?'

'Yes, I saw her,' I said cautiously.

'She would have had to close her shop in order to come. But there was no need for her presence, it wasn't required by the coroner.'

'I suppose...well, Oliver was a friend, and I suppose she felt that she ought to.'

'It's not his funeral we're talking about, Tracy, where people attend to pay their respects. Why was Mrs Kemp so anxious to hear the proceedings? She was very jumpy, wasn't she? Would you say that she's a nervous person?'

I had to admit that one wouldn't describe Ursula as nervous.

'Okay,' I said, 'so what was the outcome when you asked her about the magazine?'

'Puzzling. I made that particular call myself, yesterday afternoon. Mrs Kemp searched around vaguely, then announced that she must have thrown it out. She chatttered about building up a terrible accumulation of stuff if you aren't careful to turn things out regularly.'

'That makes sense.'

'I might have thought so, too, except for one thing. Glancing round the shop while she was supposed to be looking in her bedroom upstairs, I noticed a pile of back numbers of

151

Cotswold Illustrated. Now, if Mrs Kemp reckoned that she could make a few pence by selling them second-hand, why on earth should she have thrown away the copy in question?'

'Did you ask her?'

'No, I was anxious to avoid alerting her too much because there was something else I wanted to ask her.'

'What was that?'

Neil seemed to be considering how much to tell me. He began slowly, choosing his words, 'We've been having a look at Oliver Medway's personal bank account. It won't come as any surprise to you, I imagine, that he was frequently overdrawn?'

'No, it doesn't.'

'The credits consisted mainly of a regular monthly allowance made to him by his father, the salary he paid himself from the Design Studio, and a weekly cheque which apparently covered the business expenses he had claimed. I assume, knowing your role in the firm, that you kept a fairly close eye on Medway's spending in that direction.'

'You assume correctly. Knowing that I'd query every extravagance kept a brake on Oliver.'

Neil nodded. 'The puzzling thing about his bank account is that every now and then a considerable sum was paid in—several hundreds of pounds in one go. In cash. And usually at a time when the bank manager was getting restless about the size of his overdraft. Now where, do you think, would Oliver Medway have obtained that sort of money in banknotes?'

'His bookmaker, perhaps? He did quite a bit of betting.'

'And quite a bit of losing! But when on rare occasions he had a win, the bookie always paid by cheque.'

I shrugged. 'There must be an explanation.'

'There's an explanation for everything, Tracy. But not always a pleasant one.'

Neil was making me feel uneasy, and I couldn't quite pin down why.

'You surely aren't hinting that Oliver was some kind of thief?'

'Not in the accepted sense. But perhaps that mysterious money was payments he received in exchange for his silence.'

'You don't mean blackmail?' I gasped.

'It's a possibility we can't rule out.'

'But...but Oliver wasn't like that. He would never have...'

'I wonder how well you really knew him,' Neil interrupted. 'I'll tell you this much, Tracy, my superintendent has a full scale investigation going. And I don't just mean in and around Steeple Haslop.'

I was reduced to silence. The barman came out and cleared some empty glasses from a nearby table, made some remark about the fine weather, and disappeared inside again.'

At last I said, reluctantly, 'You mentioned Ursula earlier. You surely can't be thinking that Oliver was blackmailing *her?*'

'It's possible, though somehow I don't think it's likely.'

'So how are you trying to make a connection with Ursula?'

'There was clearly a special sort of relationship between those two. The fact that they could share a giggle over that rampant fertility god is one indication, and you've told me that he was often round at her shop. Perhaps it was a relief to Oliver Medway to have just one woman with whom he could relax, with whom he could drop the devastating seducer image and be himself.'

'He was able to do that with me,' I objected.

'You must surely see that it was different with you, Tracy. However friendly you two were, his guard would have been up to some extent because you were the watchdog put in by his father. Only a minute ago you were explaining to me how you kept a brake on his expenses, and you told me earlier about your function of preventing Medway's wilder flights of fancy and holding him down to practicalities. Yes?'

'Yes, but...'

'So if there was anyone in or around Steeple Haslop,' Neil continued smoothly, 'with whom Oliver Medway would have talked freely and let his hair down a bit, I reckoned that person was Ursula Kemp. Therefore, it seemed possible that he might have made an off-guard reference to her about someone or something in his past which would give us a clue to his killer. Mrs Kemp herself, not knowing the lines along which we are thinking, might not have attributed any special significance to such a reference. Why should she? All the same, I thought it worth doing a little digging with her.'

My pulses quickened. 'And did you discover anything?'

'Not yet. She was being very wary—some people are like that with the police, whether they have anything to hide or not.'

'So does that mean you'll be questioning her again?'

'Certainly I will. And I shall go on questioning her until I'm quite satisfied that there's no information to be extracted from that source.'

I thought for a moment. 'Does Ursula understand why you've been asking her all those questions?'

'Naturally not. Any mention of the word blackmail might make her clam up completely.'

I had never felt any strong liking for Ursula Kemp. Looking back, I recognised that there might even have been a slight antipathy in my attitude towards her, caused by the very thing Neil was talking about...her rather special relationship with Oliver. I didn't much like to acknowledge it, but I realised now that I'd taken a certain pride in thinking of myself as the *only* woman with whom Oliver had any kind of closeness that didn't involve sex.

All the same, I couldn't help feeling sorry for Ursula now because of the way she was being badgered by the police. If she was an actual a murder suspect, fair enough. But Neil was merely using her, trying to winkle out information which Ursula might not even possess. So what construction would she put on his visits? Even that one call from Neil yesterday afternoon seemed to have scared her half out of her mind.

'I'll have to be going in a minute,' I told Neil. 'There's loads of work waiting to be done.'

'Is everything settled with Sir Robert Medway now? I mean, about your taking over the Design Studio?'

'I haven't heard any more, but he said that he'd be getting his solicitor to draw up an agreement.'

'The old boy still looks in pretty bad shape,' Neil commented.

'So would you,' I said sourly, 'if you had a dicky heart and your son had just been murdered.'

'Perhaps so.' He seemed about to add something more, but thought better of it.

I'd suddenly had enough of Neil and his little chats. He pretended that I was in his confidence. But was he just using me in exactly the same way as he was using Ursula?

'Thanks for the drink,' I said, and stood up abruptly.

Neil followed suit. 'I'll just walk you back to your car.'

'There's no need.'

'But I want to, Tracy.'

As we walked the short distance to the forecourt of the municipal offices, Neil asked my opinion of the architecture of the new police headquarters which we passed on our way. Though I considered it an innocuous building, some impulse made me say, 'I think it's hideous.'

'Aesthetically, you could be right,' he granted. 'But at least it's well suited to its purpose. Care to see inside?'

I couldn't avoid a shudder, which he probably noticed.

'I told you, I've no time to spare.'

'Pity. Still, we can always make it another day. You'd be amazed, Tracy, at what goes on inside that building. Why, just on this murder enquiry alone the Chief Superintendent's got a whole team of us beavering away.'

'I'd hardly have thought,' I countered, 'that you've been beavering away this past half-hour.'

Neil grinned. 'I'd better pass that one. Anything I say in reply might be taken down and used in evidence against me.'

CHAPTER 9

There was a CLOSED card hanging behind the glass door of Ursula Kemp's shop, but it was lunch-time by now so I wasn't surprised.

I pressed the bell-push, waited, then pressed it again. After further delay the door to the private quarters at the back opened and Ursula came through. She began gesticulating that the shop was closed, then saw it was me. Reluctantly, I felt sure, she came to open up.

'Hallo, Tracy.'

'Hi! I spotted you in court this morning, Ursula, but you left so quickly that I didn't have a chance for a word. Er...am I disturbing your lunch?'

She shook her head, vaguely.

'Well then,' I said with a bright smile, 'I'll just come in for a minute or two.'

'All right.' Unenthusiastically, she stood aside and motioned me to go on through to the back.

Ursula's living room had a delightful outlook over a small, rose-trellised garden with a stream at the bottom. Her tiny kitchen was to one side, and I knew—though I'd never seen them—that there were two bedrooms and a bathroom above.

There was no sign of any lunch. Just half a cup of coffee, which appeared to have been allowed to go stone cold. Seeing Ursula nearer to, she looked quite ill, suddenly a lot older. She held her cardigan clutched about her, and I noticed that her hands were trembling. She waited in silence for me to speak.

'The verdict came as no surprise, of course,' I said, to get a conversation launched. 'I suppose that Sir Robert must be thankful to have the ordeal behind him, though he still has the funeral to face.'

Ursula gave an odd little jerky nod. Clearly she was under great strain. For a moment I even wondered if her relationship with Oliver could possibly have been closer than I'd supposed, but I dismissed the thought at once.

'Would...would you like some coffee?' she asked in a cracked voice.

I started to refuse, since I was about to go home for lunch, then it struck me that she might like a few minutes alone in the kitchen to get a grip on herself...as Cynthia Fairford had done the other day.

'Thanks,' I said. 'I could use a cup.'

While she was gone, I stood at the window

160

watching the breeze ruffling the leaves of some willow trees across the stream. Then I turned and glanced around the room. My eye was caught by a magazine on a side table. The picture on the cover was familiar, three horses taking a hurdle at Cheltenham races. I realised that it was last month's issue of *Cotswold Illustrated*. Moving across hurriedly, I picked it up and flipped through the pages. They were all intact.

Before I could put the magazine down again Ursula had returned with my coffee. There was a tinge of colour to her cheeks, and I distinctly caught a whiff of brandy. She must have taken a quick nip to steady her nerves.

Seeing what I was holding, she remarked with tight-knit brow, 'The detective inspector was here yesterday afternoon, and he asked about that magazine. I couldn't lay my hands on it at the time, then it turned up last night in my sewing cupboard.'

I was about to tell her what it was that Neil had been after; but I kept silent, a new thought clawing at my mind—or rather, an old thought that I'd dismissed before. Was Ursula Kemp the sender of that anonymous letter?

Her story about mislaying that magazine could well be true, of course; but equally, if she were guilty, she might have thought it prudent to try to get another copy of the June issue after Neil's enquiries. Perhaps this morning she had done the rounds of the newsagents in Gilchester until she found one that still had a copy of last month's number on sale. Perhaps, in fact, her attendance at the inquest had merely been a blind to cover her trip to town.

My thoughts tumbled on wildly. Neil considered it unlikely that it was Ursula who had been blackmailed by Oliver. But just suppose it *had* been her, wouldn't that constitute a motive for murder? Would Ursula have been physically capable of it? She was quite a strong woman, I'd guess, and in good health; and being well-known to Oliver she could easily have taken him by surprise. But that would mean that Ursula had left her shop in the middle of a weekday morning when it should have been open. Why not, though? The What-Not Shop wasn't like the village general store, with locals popping in and out all the time. Her trade was confined almost entirely to people passing through Steeple Haslop, tourists and trippers. Who would be likely to have noticed that for an hour or so on a wet and windswept morning Ursula Kemp's shop was in fact shut? She'd hardly have drawn attention to the fact by hanging the CLOSED sign on the door, as now.

Getting to and from the Coach House at

Haslop Hall without being seen would have been difficult for her—but possible. Madly risky, of course, but perhaps a chance worth taking for a woman driven beyond endurance.

Always supposing, I reminded myself, that Oliver was indeed a blackmailer. I realised with a jolt that I was coming to believe this, to accept it as though it were a proven fact.

'Er...sorry, Ursula, what was that?' I asked, aware that she had spoken. She was looking at me oddly, and I was afraid that my preoccupation must have been very apparent.

'I said that Inspector Grant had me searching all over the place for that magazine. Goodness knows why he should have been so keen to see it.' Her gaze was intent. Was she watching to see how I reacted, gauging whether I had been told about the anonymous letter?

I made an effort to sound casual, unconcerned. 'Neil Grant just likes to be mysterious. I expect he wanted to look up an advertisement or something.'

'Perhaps you're right,' said Ursula, not sounding as if she believed it, though.

'Have you heard that I'm going to be able to stay on at Steeple Haslop?' I babbled. 'Sir Robert invited me to take over the Design Studio.'

'I see!' Was she really listening? 'You must

be pleased, Tracy.'

'I'm delighted! Or rather, you know what I mean...I wouldn't have wanted it to happen like this, of course, but naturally I'm glad to have the chance of running my own business. I believe that I can make a go of things financially,' I added. 'I learnt a lot from Oliver, and I can put all that knowledge to good use now.'

I saw Ursula's eyes narrow in a swift, calculating glance. It had been a stupid thing for me to say, which could easily have sounded to her like a veiled threat of continuing blackmail. I felt suddenly nervous, and the cup I was holding jiggled in its saucer.

'I shall settle up your bill,' I promised, 'as soon as the bank account is freed. It shouldn't be too long now.'

Ursula made a dismissive gesture, not commenting. As her silence lengthened and she continued to watch me closely, I began to feel distinctly rattled.

'I intend to go on buying things from you whenever possible, Ursula. And you must remember to let me know if you ever come across anything you think might interest me.'

Her nod was barely discernible. Not being able to think of anything else to say to improve the atmosphere, I drank down my coffee quickly, and murmured, 'I mustn't keep you. You'll be wanting to open the shop again soon, and I've got work to do myself.'

As I turned towards the door, she said abruptly, 'Tracy, I...'

'Yes?'

I paused and glanced back at her. Ursula just stared at me, her eyes dark with pain or fear, I couldn't decide which; then slowly she shook her head.

'Nothing...it was nothing.'

'You're sure?'

She smiled faintly. 'Yes, I was just being silly. Goodbye, Tracy.'

I knew it was no use pressing her, so I said brightly, 'Thanks for the coffee.'

After a quick snack lunch at Honeysuckle Cottage, I drove to the studio. Billy Moon was out in the courtyard, hosing down the cobble-stones in front of the stables.

'That was a super ride Tim Baxter and I had on Saturday evening,' I said. 'Perhaps the two of us could go out again soon?'

Billy made no reply, nor did he return my smile. He just looked at me with a dour expression.

'By the way,' I went on, 'there's something I meant to ask you. That morning Mr Med-way was killed, did you happen to be around?'

He glared at me. 'What you getting at, miss?'

'Just...well, I wondered if perhaps you spotted anyone coming or going to the studio.'

'I were busy doing me work and minding me own business,' he said fiercely. 'That's the same as I told the coppers. I said to 'em straight out, "I'm not a man to poke his nose in where it's no right to be".'

He raised the nozzle of the hose as a sign for me to clear off. But I lingered and tried again.

'It just struck me, Billy, if someone had come along whom you knew quite well, you might hardly have taken any notice of them. But perhaps...'

'If you don't mind, miss, I've got me work to do,' he interrupted, and began to spray water around, almost splashing me. Though Billy was often taciturn, I'd never before known him to be outright rude. There was nothing for it but a dignified withdrawal. Reaching the door at the foot of the stairs, I glanced back as I fumbled with the latchkey. The old man was staring across at me, a troubled look on his weather-beaten face.

I carried the mail upstairs and glanced through it. But there was nothing that urgently needed attention. I went to my drawing board, and had another go at preparing the visuals of the thatched-barn conversion. But I

166

felt utterly devoid of inspiration. Half of my mind was wondering when Tim would contact me. On an impulse I reached for the phone and dialled his number. Having been so moody and off-putting when he'd mentioned plans for this evening, I reasoned, it was only friendly for me to take the initiative now.

'Cotswold Vintage,' he answered, after the usual long wait.

The mere sound of his voice gave me a little leap of excitement. 'Tim, this is Tracy.'

'Oh, hallo.' He sounded slightly guarded, I thought. 'I tried to get you a couple of times... both at the studio and at home. Where've you been?'

Not wanting to tell him about having a drink with Neil, I said, 'I had various things to do. I slipped home for a few minutes just now though, and snatched a bite to eat. About this evening...we didn't really settle anything, did we?'

'That's what I wanted to explain, Tracy. I just remembered my VAT return. It's a curse, but it's already a few days overdue and it must be done...they won't give you the slightest leeway. So I'm afraid this evening is out.'

It was absurd for me to feel so slapped down. But I did, and I bitterly regretted that I'd phoned him.

'Oh, that's okay,' I lied. 'Don't give it another thought.'

'About tomorrow...' Tim began, but I chopped him off short. 'I'm not sure about tomorrow. Give me a ring sometime, if you like, and I'll see.'

'Right then,' he said briskly, and rang off. I knew that I was being unfair in blaming him, but I couldn't help it. I tried to look at the facts plainly...Tim was a hard-working wine grower whose life during the summer amounted to a running battle against everything nature could throw at him. So it was perfectly understandable that he should have thrust aside boring and inessential bookwork until the very last moment, and then nearly have forgotten about it altogether in all this business of Oliver's death and having to go to court this morning. If the Design Studio's VAT return had been due this month, I might well have been in the same boat myself. But such reasonable arguments did nothing to sweeten my acid mood.

Bleakness really hit me during the evening. Before I'd always enjoyed my cottage, never being averse to spending a quiet, relaxed evening at home. But now I couldn't settle down to anything. I was a fool to take this petulant attitude, and Tim must think me impossibly touchy. Should I phone him and apologise?

I switched off the radio in the middle of a book programme and went out to the phone in the hall; hesitated, picked it up, hesitated again, and dialled his number. Tim didn't answer at once, though, and I let it go on ringing. But still there was no answer—very odd. I let it ring for a long while before I finally gave up and put the phone down.

It was Mrs Sparrow who brought the news next morning. Arriving earlier than usual— while I was still having breakfast—she was full of breathless excitement.

'Have you heard about the accident, Miss Yorke?'

'What accident?'

Gratified that she'd not been forestalled, she spun out her pleasure by keeping me waiting while she removed her coat and donned a flowered apron.

'It's that there Mrs Kemp at the What-Not Shop! Last night she went and run off the road in her car.'

'Oh dear!' I exclaimed. 'Is she badly hurt?'

Elsie Sparrow tied the tapes of her apron with a dramatic flourish.

'She's not *hurt*, dear, she's dead!'

Horror surged over me, and with it came a

dozen darting images. Ursula's face in the coroner's court, and again when I'd called on her afterwards, drawn and tense and...yes, frightened. Then, the brandy she'd taken to steady her nerves. Neil's questioning had obviously shaken her badly...because she was guilty? Guilty of sending a slanderous letter? Guilty of murder? Or both? I recalled her last words to me, just as I was leaving. She had seemed on the brink of saying something important, but she hadn't been quite able to bring it out. Would it have been a sort of confession?

'How did it happen?' I asked Mrs Sparrow on a catch of breath. 'Where was Mrs Kemp going?'

'There's no one to tell us that now, dear, is there?'

'Weren't there any witnesses?'

'Seems not. It happened on the little road along the top of Soulter's Ridge, you see. That stretch of road is very quiet...Mrs Kemp couldn't have chosen a lonelier spot round hereabouts if she'd been trying. Young Steve Gardner it was who found her, on his way to work this morning...you know the lad I mean, Harry Gardner's boy, the cowman over at Bailey's Farm. He spotted the tyre marks going off the road, and the fence at the side was all smashed, so he got off his motor bike and looked down over the edge. He could just see the car lying upside down with its wheels in the air, right at the very bottom. Almost buried in the trees, it was.'

'What...what do the police have to say?' I asked, feeling a bit faint.

'Well, I mean...what can they say, 'cepting it was a shocking accident? Mrs Kemp weren't what you could call a drinker, was she? Not to my knowledge, anyways, and you usually gets to know these things in a village. If you ask me, she had a burst tyre or something just at the wrong moment, and over she went to her death, poor soul.'

Suicide? The word was battering at my mind. Had Ursula Kemp, believing that the police were closing in on her, killed herself as the only way of escape? Every second that passed, I became more and more convinced of it.

So what did I do? Leave well alone and let her death be recorded, decently, as an accident? Let the sordid truth be buried with her?

Perhaps there was no need for me to intervene, I reflected. Perhaps the police knew more than I thought they knew, or they would find evidence at the spot that the crash had been deliberate. Be that as it may, I knew that I had a duty to pass on my suspicions...Neil had drummed this into me, and I'd already been in enough trouble with him without risking more.

Elsie Sparrow was chattering on. 'I heard that Mrs Kemp was at the inquest yesterday morning. They say she looked proper poorly... all white and upset.' A knowingness crept into her voice. 'She had a very soft spot for young Mr Medway, I reckon...a bit over fond of him, like. Aren't I right?'

'That's absolute nonsense,' I said, trying to stop myself from sounding shrill. 'We often used to buy things from her shop and she and Oliver were friendly, that's all it ever was.'

'If you say so,' nodded Mrs Sparrow with sage disbelief. 'The way it struck me, though, was that if his death had upset her very bad, like...well, that could've accounted for her losing control of her car. Not properly thinking about what she was doing, if you see what I mean.'

I said, less than coherently. 'Well, anyone can be upset when...when a friend is *murdered*. It doesn't mean that Mrs Kemp...'

Mrs Sparrow allowed my babbling to pass her by. 'I wonder where she was going, at that time of night?'

'What time of night?' I asked quickly. 'Is it known when the accident actually happened?'

'Well, it must've been latish, stands to reason. After dark for sure, otherwise the fence and all that would've been noticed sooner. And that means sometime from about ten o'clock on. So, where would she have been going, d'you reckon?'

'Going home after a visit somewhere, I imagine.'

'No, that's what makes it so peculiar. She was driving *away* from home.'

I didn't intend to phone Neil in Mrs Sparrow's hearing. Telling her that I wanted to get to the studio early this morning, I hastily put my breakfast things into the sink and left. She was disappointed, I knew, having reckoned to spin out the interesting speculation over a cup of coffee. Doubtless she was hoping that my close association with Oliver would throw up a gossipy titbit.

I rang Neil the instant I got to the studio. He wasn't in, though, and I refused to talk to anyone else. So I had to leave a message for him to call me back, and the hour or so that passed before he rang seemed like an age.

'You wanted me, Tracy?'

Stupidly, now that he was on the line I suddenly became choked with doubt. A few odd suspicions strung together didn't turn an accident into suicide...a suicide motivated

173

by a murder.

'Neil...it was just...about the accident to Ursula Kemp. I suppose you've heard about it?'

'I most certainly have.'

'Well...' How on earth did I begin?

'You've got something on your mind, Tracy?'

'I'm not really sure, but...'

Neil made a swift decision. 'I'm coming straight over. You're at the studio, are you?'

'Yes.' I was glad, now, that there was no going back.

As I waited for him, making meaningless squiggles on paper, I suddenly remembered a job I'd completely forgotten about. At once I phoned the contractors who were supposed to be working on the consulting rooms of the chiropractor in Cheltenham. To my intense relief I learned that they'd started the job yesterday, and that so far there'd been no snags. Thank God for that!

When I heard Neil's car in the courtyard, I went to the head of the staircase to greet him. He ran up and took hold of me by the shoulders, studying my face.

'Now then, what's all this about?' he demanded. 'On the phone you sounded in a bit of a dither.'

I came out with it in a rush of words. 'Ursula Kemp's accident...do you think it could possibly have been suicide?'

'Anything is possible, love,' he said. 'I thought I'd already taught you that lesson. You'd better give me your reasons for thinking it was suicide.'

'I'm not sure that I *do*. It's just...'

'Why not sit down,' he suggested, 'then talk?'

He himself perched on the edge of my table, facing me, while I began uncertainly. 'After driving back from the inquest yesterday, I called in on Ursula, and she was in a very odd mood.'

'*Why* did you call on her?'

I looked up and met his gaze. 'Because I thought that you were being rather tough on her, Neil. I mean, even though you didn't really suspect Ursula, you were putting pressure on her to try and extract information about Oliver. I reckoned it must have really upset her. You said yourself how desperate she looked in court, so I thought I'd...'

'Tracy, you weren't intending to pass on to her what I'd told you in confidence?'

'Of course I wasn't! I was just...I don't quite know what I intended to do. I felt sorry for her, and it was an impulse. Ursula hadn't many friends, you see, and she was obviously taking Oliver's death very hard.'

Neil smiled wryly. 'You're too soft-hearted. So what happened?'

'Well, while she was making me some coffee, I noticed a copy of *Cotswold Illustrated* lying on a table...last month's issue. I took a quick look at it, and all the pages were intact.'

'Interesting!'

'Yes. Anyway, Ursula saw that I'd picked it up, and she told me that you had been asking her about it the day before, but that she couldn't find it. She said that it had turned up later in her sewing cupboard.'

'So then?'

I made a helpless little gesture with my hands. 'I know it must sound stupid, but an idea suddenly hit me. It all fitted in with the terrible state Ursula was in at the inquest, and she still was when I called round to see her. I suddenly thought—suppose she *had* sent that anonymous letter? After you asked her about the magazine she might have reasoned that she'd better get hold of last month's issue to cover up her tracks. She *could* have bought it somewhere in Gilchester on Mondy morning.'

Neil was thoughtful. 'Why should she send a nasty letter about you, Tracy? Did she have something against you?'

176

'No, I'm sure she didn't. Ursula never showed the least sign of disliking me, or in any way resenting me. But it could have been just to divert suspicion from herself. She knew how vital it was for me to establish that I'd driven through the village at twelve-fifteen and not any earlier.'

'How did she know that?'

'Because I told her—the day after Oliver was killed.'

'So what you're saying is that you think it was Ursula Kemp who killed Oliver Medway? Presumably because he was blackmailing her?'

'Well...yes.'

'Tell me, Tracy, how did you make the surprising deduction that Mrs Kemp killed herself?'

As I had dreaded Neil was pouring scorn on my ideas. But I couldn't back-pedal now.

'Doesn't it all add up?' I argued. 'The way I see it is that when you questioned her on Sunday about the magazine, Ursula must have thought you were suspicious of her—not guessing that it was just a routine enquiry. And at the same time you asked her a lot of probing questions about Oliver, too. So my guess is that she was really scared by then. She would have known that the police always follow things through. So if you started delving into her past—before she came to Steeple Haslop—you would soon turn up whatever it was she wanted to keep hidden so desperately that Oliver was able to blackmail her because of it. When that happened, the game would be up. So her only chance was to make a run for it—or to give up and kill herself.'

'What a tissue of supposition,' Neil remarked, after a moment.

'Which means that you think it's all a load of rubbish?'

'I think it's an interesting hypothesis,' he said.

'But you don't believe it for one second?'

He slid off his perch on the table and wandered over to the window, staring out across the river as if debating how much to tell me. Eventually, he turned to face me again.

'I think the suggestion that Ursula Kemp committed suicide is considerably more likely than that her death was accidental.'

I was astonished to hear Neil agreeing with me, and I couldn't help feeling a bit triumphant.

'Does this mean that you've found some evidence to suggest it was suicide?' I asked him.

'Nothing definite. But in my job you develop a "nose".'

'You still have doubts, though?'

Neil stood there with a deep frown on his face. I had a feeling that he was mentally sorting through the few facts and the mass of supposition about Ursula's death.

He said slowly, 'There's a third possibility, Tracy.'

My skin prickled. 'You...you mean that someone...?'

He nodded. 'If that accident was faked, if it was murder made to *look* like an accident, that puts a whole new complexion on things, doesn't it?'

CHAPTER 10

In the oak-beamed refectory at Haslop Hall everyone was busy talking about the weather. What a blessing it was fine, we all said. How much more depressing an occasion this funeral would seem had it been a wet day...like the day Oliver was—no one could quite bring himself to actually use the word.

Earlier, in the little Saxon church dedicated to St Gregory, the vicar had conducted the service to a capacity congregation. The Reverend Peter Anders was a modern young churchman who, so I'd heard, was wont to have straight man-to-man chats about sex with embarrassed youth club members, and daily downed his jolly pint in the bar of the Trout Inn. He was here now, gravely enjoying the good amontillado provided by Sir Robert while he circuited the room exchanging a few polite words with each guest. I watched him move inexorably towards the corner where I stood with Tim.

'Hallo, you two. What a tragic business this is! And now we have another fatality in our little community. Poor lady! Still, we must be thankful, I suppose, that her passing was not attended with the same hideous brutality as with Mr Medway. What a monster the assassin must be!'

I had been forbidden by Neil to give the slightest hint of his suspicions concerning Ursula's death. For the time being, he'd adjured me, it must continue to be regarded as an accident. So I made suitable concurring noises until the vicar felt his duty to us had been done.

'That chap almost trips over his own exclamation marks,' Tim commented, as he moved out of earshot.

'He works hard,' I said. 'You've got to grant him that.'

The guests, each in turn, had mumbled a few conventional words of condolence to Sir Robert upon arriving at the Hall, after which everyone seemed very content to steer clear of him. The poor man was seated in an upright chair to one side of the massive carved mantel, Sebastian hovering at his elbow. Oliver's father had borne himself with dignity throughout the ordeal at the church, but now he looked drained, scarcely aware of what was going on around him. His fighting spirit seemed to have evaporated completely. Perhaps, I reflected, he felt that he could give up now that his heir was the virtuous Sebastian.

Lady Medway, mourning with elegance in an expensive black silk dress, was conscientiously moving from one group to another. Or did she find this preferable to being in the company of her husband? I realised that I'd not seen them exchange as much as a single word this morning.

Tim, observing her reach out for another glass of sherry from the circulating Grainger's tray, remarked, 'Lady M is tanking up, isn't she? That must be her fifth or sixth.'

Yesterday had gone by without Tim and me managing to patch things up. But today, when he came and sat down beside me in the church, a truce had tacitly been declared between us for the duration of the funeral.

Diana Medway was bearing down on us, a little unsteadily but still in fair control.

'You're a sly one, Tracy!' she said.

'I'm sorry, Lady Medway, I don't understand.'

'No?' She flickered a meaningful glance at Tim. 'This is the "friend" you took riding with you, I hear. It didn't take you long, did it?'

She meant, to find myself a replacement for Oliver. And I had to stand there meekly and take it. I could hardly start a slanging match right here in her own house on the day of her stepson's funeral.

Tim, bless him, spiked her guns with an easy smile. 'You didn't object to me using one of your horses, did you, Lady Medway?'

She lifted her slender shoulders in an elaborate shrug.

'I haven't the least objection,' she drawled, 'so long as you know what you're doing.'

'Oh yes, I can assure you that I do know what I'm doing.'

Diana Medway stared at him coldly, but decided not to follow that through.

'As I told Tracy the other day,' she said, with another elegantly performed shrug, 'those horses need exercising.'

Tim observed with amusement as she tacked off across the room, 'What a flaming bitch that woman is.'

'She's been in a very peculiar mood lately,' I said. 'I just don't know what to make of it. Her attitude to me was always distant, but on Saturday, when she stopped me and suggested that I should keep up the riding, she was suddenly very pally. Then today...'

Tim nodded. Then, 'She seems to have taken against her husband, doesn't she? In church this morning you could almost hear a wind whistling through the gap between the two of them.'

'Why don't you go over and talk to Sir Robert?' I found myself suggesting. 'It's awful the way everyone is avoiding him. You might be able to cheer him up a bit.'

'Think so?'

'Besides, it's an opportunity to get to know Sebastian. And you'll have to be on closer terms with him, won't you, now that he's the new heir?'

'True,' he said. 'Are you coming with me?'

I shook my head. Actually, I had decided that I'd better go and confront Ralph and Grace. So far I'd only been awarded a freezing nod, as at the inquest, and I reckoned it was time to heal the breach.

My opportunity came a moment later when the little knot of people with whom the Ebborns had been chatting, a couple of tenant farmers and their wives, broke up. I went across to waylay them, and came straight to the point.

'Look, I know that you're blaming me for telling the police about Sebastian, but I *had* to, you must see that.'

'You promised us that you'd leave it to Ralph,' said Grace, tight-lipped with resentment.

'Yes, and I meant to at the time—even though it went against my conscience. But when I got talking to Neil Grant and he asked me about Sebastian...well, I'd have been withholding information from the police if I hadn't admitted what I knew.'

'You've become very thick with that detective inspector,' Ralph said.

'Neil Grant,' I pointed out, trying to keep my temper, 'is someone I've know ever since the time I first came to live in Steeple Haslop. You're not suggesting for heaven's sake, that the police should be treated as The Enemy, and ostracised?'

Ralph made a bitter face at me. 'All that your interference has achieved, Tracy, is to stir up a lot of unnecessary trouble for Sebastian. The police have been badgering him with endless questions and checking up on his movements. I can tell you that he's damned annoyed about it, and he holds you entirely to blame.'

'Oh! So you told him that the information came from me, did you?'

'Naturally I did. Sebastian will be my employer one day—and it could be any day now, considering the precarious state of Sir Robert's health. I just couldn't afford to have him thinking that I'd gone sneaking behind his back talking about him to the police.'

Even if I granted that Ralph had a point, this was a murder enquiry, dammit. I'd only done what I had to do, and it was too late for regrets.

'Why did you tell me,' I asked him, injecting challenge into my voice, 'that Sebastian had given you a completely satisfactory explanation for being in the district last Wednesday morning?'

Ralph gave me an odd glance. 'Because he did, Tracy.'

'The police don't agree,' I said.

'What exactly is that supposed to mean?' he demanded sharply.

I sighed. 'Perhaps I shouldn't really be saying this, but Neil Grant told me that Sebastian isn't automatically cleared by the explanation he gave them.'

Ralph was staring at me in horror; Grace in plain bewilderment.

'Are you telling me,' he spluttered, 'that the police seriously think that Sebastian'—he dropped his voice to an almost inaudible manner—'killed Oliver?'

'Not at all, but they're keeping an open mind. I gather that his alibi isn't completely watertight.' I paused a moment, then asked, 'What *was* the explanation he gave you, Ralph?'

'I can't tell you that,' he replied sourly. 'But

I'm surprised that Inspector Grant didn't, since you seem to be so completely in the man's confidence.'

To my relief, I saw that Tim was coming over, weaving his way through the little clusters of people standing around with their sherry glasses and buffet snacks. He was looking pleased about something, I decided, and I wondered what it was. After a couple of minutes of strained conversation with Ralph and Grace, he gave them a good-natured smile, and deftly steered me away.

'Well,' I asked him, 'how did you get on with Sir Robert?'

'It all worked out rather nicely, Tracy. Without any prompting from me the question of a long-term lease on the vineyard came up, and the old boy isn't at all opposed to my ideas. Even more to the point, neither is Sebastian.'

'I'm glad for you, Tim.'

It had been my suggestion that Tim should cement relations with Sebastian, and the outcome could hardly have been more favourable. But would Sebastian Medway ever be in a position to implement any promises he might make to Tim or anyone else concerning the future of the Haslop Hall estate? I wondered if the police had checked on his whereabouts on the night of Ursula's death.

'You don't *sound* very glad,' Tim commented, and gave me a measuring stare. 'What were
the solemn looks between you and the Ebborns
in aid of?'

'You're imagining things,' I said lightly.

'Tracy, Tracy! Who are you trying to fool?'

The less important, non-family guests were
beginning to depart. As Tim and I went to take
our leave of the Medways, I was aware of something unexpected in Sebastian's attitude to me.
I'd dreaded an angry, challenging glare; but
instead he seemed to avoid meeting my eyes.
I became aware, with something of a shock,
that Sebastian Medway was half afraid of
me.

'I would have suggested that we have some
lunch together,' said Tim. 'But after all those
nibbly bits they laid on...'

'Count me out,' I said hastily. 'I'm full.'

We were standing beside Tim's car. Not to
add to the inevitable crush on the circle of
gravel outside the Hall, I'd left my Fiesta over
by the Coach House. People passing nodded
goodbye to us, their glances registering the fact
that we were together.

'About this evening, then,' Tim persisted.
'Shall I see you?'

'Do you fancy another ride?' I asked him

after a flick of thought. I wouldn't be committing myself to too much, this way, and there would be less chance of another prickly situation developing between us.

'I'd like that, Tracy. Her ladyship wasn't very gracious, but she did give us permission.'

'And it's perfectly true that the horses need to be exercised,' I added.

'So we've talked ourselves into it. What time do you suggest?'

'Would six o'clock be too early? I'll drop in on my way to the studio now and soften up Billy Moon a bit.'

With his car door open, Tim paused and looked at me.

'Why should Billy Moon need to be softened up?'

'I don't know why.' Rashly, against my better judgment, I went on, 'For some reason he seems to be down on you, Tim.'

'Oh? What's the old chap been saying about me?'

'Nothing, really. It's just the impression I got.'

Tim laughed. 'Well, you tell him that he couldn't hope to meet a nicer bloke than Timothy Baxter, not in a month of Sundays.'

I was about to make a flip retort, but I had a feeling that Tim wasn't really amused.

Everything was quiet when I reached the stables. The horses would all be out in the paddocks. I wandered into the tack room, hoping to find Billy there. It was also his den, where he would sit puffing his pipe in reflective moments. I was out of luck, though.

As always, like every square inch of the territory under Billy Moon's command, the little room was spotless; the floor well-swept, each piece of tack hung in its appointed place, the wooden saddle-horse scrubbed, the saddles themselves placed neatly on their racks. Smiling to myself, I took a ball-point and a scrap of paper from my shoulderbag to leave Billy a note.

There was a high, old-fashioned counting-house desk which had probably been relegated here at some long-ago time when the estate offices were modernised. Under its sloping lid, I knew, was a meticulously-kept stable log book written up in Billy's spidery script. On the match-boarding wall above this, fixed with drawing pins, was a calendar from a feed firm, a faded picture postcard of Blackpool Tower, a poster concerning some horse trials at Cirencester, and further along...

The wave of shock passed right through me, setting my pulse throbbing. Pinned at each corner with perfect precision was a familiar coloured picture of three horses taking a hurdle at Cheltenham races. The cover of last month's *Cotswold Illustrated*.

I stepped closer, but there was no mistake. The picture had been carefully trimmed, with the magazine's title cut away. I started to lever out the drawing pins with my fingernails; gave up, searched and found a penknife with a broken handle, and used that. When I had the square of art paper off the wall I held it in my hands and stared at it hard, back and front, as if it might of itself somehow reveal a secret.

I heard a footstep outside, and swung round.

'What you a'doing, miss?' demanded Billy Moon from the doorway, sounding truculent.

I held up the picture. 'What's this, Billy? Where did you get it?'

He shuffled forward a foot or two, but not very close. 'I ain't done nothing wrong, miss, and it's no good you trying to make out that I have.'

'No, I'm sure you haven't, Billy. Only... please just tell me where it came from.'

'I found it, didn't I?'

'Found it! Where?'

'It were chucked away,' he grunted.

'Yes, but where? Was it the whole magazine you found, or just this one page?'

'All cut about it were, and no good to anyone.

191

You ain't got no cause to make an almighty fuss about it, Miss Yorke.'

I wanted to shake the information out of him. Instead, I said mildly, 'I'm not blaming you for anything, Billy. I just want you to tell me where you found the magazine. It's very important for me to know.'

He gave me a stubborn, bitter look. 'In the stable. Behind one of the mangers.'

'Show me, please.'

Grumbling to himself, Billy led the way into the big stable, which was used to house all four of the horses now kept. We walked along to the end stall, and he pointed sullenly at the manger.

'It were there, miss, stuffed right down behind. It had been throwed out, anyone could tell that. All the pages were cut about, and...'

'Where's the rest of the magazine?' I demanded excitedly.

Billy glowered at me, as if he thought that I was off my rocker. 'It's gone now, I s'pose.'

'Gone where?'

'With the rubbish, a'course. What would I want with keeping it for?'

'In the dustbins, you mean? The same ones I use for the studio?'

'I allus use them bins,' he said, now on the defensive about this new aspect. 'Nobody ain't never told me not to.'

I was already half out of the door. As I ran across the courtyard, I heard Billy call after me, 'It ain't no good you looking, miss. Them bins was emptied yesterday. We're done on a Tuesday round here.'

I still went to look, though. The two bins were indeed empty, except for a baked-bean tin and a newspaper that Billy must have thrown in since the refuse collection. He came across and stood beside me, perversely satisfied.

'I told you, miss, didn't I? Why don't you listen?'

My mind raced frantically.

'When exactly was it that you found the copy of *Cotswold Illustrated?*' I asked.

Billy's lined face creased into even more wrinkles.

'Monday, I reckon...yes, Monday art'noon. I noticed the manger pulled out a bit from the wall...that there Prince is a proper messy feeder, always jerking things about. It were when I went to shove it back that I spotted the magazine.'

'Who could have put it there, Billy?'

'How should I know?'

'Well then—who might have come in here?'

He scratched his ear. 'Anyone, I s'pose. There's only her ladyship and Mr Sebastian who do any riding these days, 'cepting for yourself, miss. But neither of them was here on Monday, 'cause of that there inquest. I didn't see no sign of anyone all day, just you on your way up to the studio.'

There was nothing more to be got out of him, that was clear.

I said, 'Well, thank you, Billy—thank you very much. I'll keep the picture, if you don't mind. And please don't say anything about this to anyone.'

'Ain't nothing to say,' he groused, half to himself. 'All this blessed hullabaloo over some old magazine nobody wanted! I only kept the picture 'cause one of they jockeys was the grandson of a bloke I used to know. But if you want to take it away from me, Miss Yorke, I can't stop you.'

'I'll get you another one, Billy,' I promised him soothingly. 'In fact, you can have the cover picture from my own copy. How's that?'

Whether he attributed it to my gender, my social class, or my character, he patently thought that I was stark raving mad.

'You do as you please, miss,' he said with a sniff. 'I got work to get on with.'

I hurried across to the studio, unlocked the door, and ran upstairs. Picking up the phone, I dialled the number of the Gilchester police

194

headquarters, and impatiently counted off the seconds that I had to wait.

'Detective Inspector Grant, please.'

'I'll see if he's in, madam. Who's speaking?'

'Miss Yorke.'

Neil came on the line immediately. 'What's new, Tracy?'

'Something important. The magazine has turned up.'

'That's something I didn't expect. Where was it?'

I explained briefly, and Neil asked several questions until he had extracted everything I knew myself. Then he said, 'I'm coming straight over. I suppose you've handled that cover page, Tracy?'

'Well, yes...'

'And Billy Moon's prints will be plastered all over it, too. I don't expect there's a hope in hell we'll find anything useful, but you never know.'

This time, while I waited for Neil to turn up, it wasn't in the same mood of nervous trepidation as before. This was not just guesswork on my part, but solid fact. Could it be that my discovery would unlock the answers to everything...the sender of the anonymous letter, Oliver's killer and—if Neil was right—Ursula's killer, too?

Neil arrived like a whirlwind. 'Okay, where's this magazine cover you found?'

I pointed to it on my table, and he studied it thoughtfully for a moment. Then, touching only the edges, he slid it into a polythene bag he took from his jacket pocket.

'Now, Tracy, I'm off to see Billy Moon. But I want you to stay here by the phone, because I'm hoping for a call to say that the remnants of the magazine have been found. If it comes through, then take the message and come down and let me know at once.'

I gaped at him in surprise. 'But how can you hope to find the rest of that magazine?'

'Luckily the council here doesn't incinerate its rubbish,' Neil explained. 'Instead, everything is dumped in an old quarry. And as the magazine in question was only in yesterday's collection, it won't be buried too deep. Chief Superintendent Blackley has sent a gang of our chaps to start sifting through the tip.' He grinned. 'Not a very savoury job for a summer's day, I'm afraid, but necessary. Let's hope, for their sake, that they find what they're looking for quickly.'

It was very silent in the studio as I waited. Unable to settle to work, I wandered through into the flat and gazed down through one of the windows overlooking the courtyard. I wondered what was happening in the stable. I had a feeling that Neil wasn't often defeated, but I doubted if he'd often met up with anyone as stubbornly unresponsive as Billy Moon could be when he felt so inclined.

Fifteen minutes later, back in the studio, I heard Neil's footsteps on the staircase. He looked gloomy as he came in and threw himself down on one of the red leather chairs.

'No phone call yet, I presume?'

I shook my head. 'How did you get on with Billy?'

'He's a right awkward old cuss, isn't he? He seems to take a positive delight in being as bloody-minded as possible. I threatened him with unnamed horrors, cajoled him, appealed to his sense of civic duty, even appealed to his vanity as being the clever chap who had found the clue that could solve the whole case for us. Useless! He just repeats, "I've telled you everything I knows, and I can't tell you nothing more." '

'Doesn't it occur to you that this might be the truth?'

Neil scuffed the carpet with the toe of his shoe. 'Oh yes, Tracy, it occurs to me. Maybe it damned well is the truth.'

'But that detective's nose of yours says not?'

He nodded. 'Quite a strong whiff, I'm getting. Still, we'll have to try other directions. Let's hope that the magazine provides us with a clue when it's dug out of the garbage tip.'

'You're hoping to find fingerprints, are you?'

'With any luck. Or there might be something else to help us identify whose copy it was.'

'What, for instance?'

Neil shrugged. 'A scribbled marginal note, maybe. Something underlined. Or something missing.'

'Something missing? What would that prove? There will be lots of bits of it missing.'

'Yes, but it's a matter of *which* bits,' he said mysteriously.

As if on cue, the phone rang. I grabbed it up quickly.

'Miss Yorke? This is Detective Sergeant Willis. Is Mr Grant there, please?'

'Yes, one moment.'

I handed Neil the phone. The sergeant's voice crackled, just below the level of audibility.

'That's splendid!' said Neil, after a moment. 'Exactly what have you got, and what's missing?'

He jotted down some figures on an envelope lying on the table, then said, 'Okay, Dave. Get things moving, will you? I'll meet you back at the station in half an hour.'

'Well?' I demanded, as he hung up.

'They've found a magazine, as you'll have guessed. It had come apart at the staples, which isn't surprising after going through garbage disposal. Luckily, though, they've managed to unearth all of it except for one sheet. Give me that copy of yours, will you? I want to have a look.'

I fished out the magazine from a drawer and handed it over.

'Let's see now,' said Neil, flipping through. 'Pages seventeen and eighteen, then fifty-seven and fifty-eight.' He found the pages concerned, which together formed a single sheet, glancing at each in turn. Then he passed the magazine back to me. 'Thanks, Tracy.'

'Did you spot anything significant?'

'Could be,' he said.

'What is it, then? Or aren't you going to tell me?'

'You won't like it much if I do.'

'Oh, come on,' I said impatiently.

'Okay. Take a look at page fifty-eight.'

I did so, and I didn't need to ask him any more. It was the page that carried the advertisement for Cotswold Vintage.

CHAPTER 11

I forced myself to get down to work after Neil's departure, but for all I achieved I might just as well not have bothered. I made a thorough botch of preparing some rough visuals for the simplest of jobs, a playroom/bedroom for twin girls aged seven. Pushing this aside in despair, I tried to do the costings for another enquiry we'd had—the remodelling of a former tobacconist's shop that was reopening as a boutique —but the figures refused to make any sense.

I heard a car entering the courtyard through the archway, and stirred myself, wondering who it might be. The sound of Tim's voice calling up the stairs jolted me. I'd forgotten all about our arrangement to go riding, and I wasn't ready to face him yet. If I ever would be again.

'Tracy! Are you up there?'

I went to the head of the stairs. 'Hallo, Tim.'

'What's the matter?' he asked, looking puzzled. 'The stables are all shut up, and you're not even changed.'

'I'm sorry,' I stammered. 'I...'

He came on upstairs, frowning. 'Did old Billy Moon turn curmudgeony or something and refuse to let us have the horses?'

I shook my head, too confused to know what to say.

Tim grinned at me lopsidedly. 'I do believe that you clean forgot about our going for a ride this evening.'

'Yes, I'm afraid I did. It went completely out of my mind.'

'Not very flattering to me!'

'Sorry,' I said again, helplessly.

Tim stepped closer and put a hand under my chin, giving a hard, penetrating look. 'There's something wrong, isn't there? Aren't you feeling well, Tracy?'

'I'm okay. It's just that all this business is getting to me. Oliver and Ursula and...and everything.'

'Everything?' Tim's mouth went taut. 'Are you still bothered about that anonymous letter?'

I looked away from him, unable to find an answer.

'I reckon you need to get out in the fresh air,' he said, 'like I've been all afternoon. It's a marvellous tonic after a gloomy funeral. If we can't have a ride, let's go walking on the hills. How about driving over to Painswick, and

201

climbing the beacon there?'

I hesitated. Part of me frantically wished Tim gone, yet I knew that I still wanted to spend the evening with him. Should I allow Neil Grant to sow seeds of suspicion in my mind, when I *knew* that Tim had nothing to do with that anonymous letter? The best thing was not to think about it at all, not to allow the insidious seeds any space to sprout.

'All right then,' I agreed. 'Just give me a couple of minutes.'

When I returned, having slipped on my black velvet jacket, I said yet again, 'Sorry about messing up our ride, Tim. It was stupid of me.'

'Don't give it another thought.' There was a pause, then he said, 'Seen anything of Neil Grant lately?'

I felt like telling him no, but I could so easily be caught out in such a silly lie.

'Well, yes...as a matter of fact he was here this afternoon.'

'Isn't the bloody man ever going to leave us alone?'

'Us? Has he been to see you again, too?'

Tim nodded. 'Yesterday afternoon.'

In Tim's estate car, we headed out of the grounds by way of the Home Farm gates. A few moments later, I realised that we were at the crossroads where Grace had seen Sebastian driving a Volvo. I gave a little shudder, wondering whether it really was Sebastian who had killed Oliver. The idea didn't bear thinking about, but it was infinitely preferable to the thought that Tim was involved.

Tim flicked me a glance, and saw my downcast face. 'Cheer up, Tracy. Shall we stop off for a drink somewhere?'

'If you like.'

He chose a little dormer-windowed pub where the beer was drawn from the wood. The two or three other customers gathered in the bar made it the hub of this lost little Cotswold hamlet almost totally buried in a wooded dell. Tim and I carried our drinks outside and sat together on a rustic bench in the full flood of evening sunshine.

'On a fine summer evening in the heart of rural England, what better than a tankard of good honest beer?' he said.

I felt myself slowly relaxing. The alcohol was smoothing off the edges of my anxiety and the sun was drenching me with warmth. Tim's shoulder touched mine, and I could have stayed there for a long time, dreamily content.

It was several minutes before Tim broke the silence, and his words shattered my mood.

'What was it that Neil Grant wanted to see you about this afternoon?'

'Just routine questions,' I said, shrugging.

For a moment or two he fiddled with his glass tankard.

'I think you're holding out on me, Tracy. Have the police formed any new theories yet?'

'I told you before, Neil wouldn't tell me if they had,' I said, forgiving myself the lie.

'What does he have to say about Ursula Kemp's accident?'

I felt cornered and it must have showed in the spikiness of my voice. 'Why should you suppose Neil has *anything* to say about it?'

'No reason. Come to think of it, he probably wouldn't deal with traffic accidents. When's the inquest?'

'How should I know? You seem to be very interested.'

He tilted his head. 'I just wondered.'

Why did Tim have to thrust to the forefront of my mind what I'd been trying to dismiss as irrelevant...that on the night of Ursula's death, when he was supposed to be at home working on his tax return, he hadn't answered when I phoned him, though I'd held on for ages. I hadn't dared to reveal this fact to Neil.

Should I challenge Tim now? I decided on a sideways approach.

'Did you get your VAT return finished on Monday evening?'

'Eventually! I'm not the world's greatest bookkeeper, even with the aid of a pocket calculator.'

I kept my voice carefully casual. 'It must seem unfair, having paperwork to do after a hard day's slog in the vineyard. I expect you felt like chucking the whole lot into the waste-bin and saying to hell with it.'

Tim laughed. 'I was tempted, I don't mind telling you. Especially when it got to midnight and the wretched columns still wouldn't tally.'

I felt my skin prickle. 'You mean to say that you worked through the entire evening, without a break?'

'It's not my style, Tracy, I agree. But I'd hate to have the Customs and Excise people descend on me. I'd be a marked man for ever more.' He drank down the last of his beer. 'Shall we go?'

But then Tim couldn't find his keys, and he fished around in each of his pockets. I finally retrieved the bunch from a tuft of grass beneath the rustic bench.

'You'll lose them completely one of these days, the way you're always leaving them around.' My eye was caught by a little chased-silver medallion attached to the ring, shaped a bit like a spade. 'What's this meant to be?'

Tim laughed. 'I've no idea, but I was assured

205

it was a potent good-luck charm. I bought it at a street market in a small village in the Loire valley, when I was grape-picking in France. The silversmith made it for me on the spot—it's a unique piece.'

I had a feeling that I'd seen one very like it before, and not long ago. Still, if Tim thought it was unique, there was no need to disillusion him.

We drove on to the foot of Painswick Beacon, and then started to walk. On this lofty vantage point with its magnificent views across the Severn valley, the farthest reaches lost now in the lilac haze of the balmy July evening, I should have felt happy. I should have felt happy just to be walking anywhere with Tim because I knew how important he was to me. But too many shadows were lurking in my mind.

'What shall we do about food?' Tim asked, as we stood on a small knot looking westwards towards the sunset.

'I'm not really hungry,' I said.

'Well, I am! And you ought to eat, whether you feel like it or not. So how about volunteering to cook us a meal at home?'

'I haven't anything in.'

'Not even bacon and eggs?'

'I suppose so.'

'Great! There's nothing I'd enjoy more.'

It was dusk when we reached Honeysuckle Cottage. After we had eaten we sat over coffee with the lovely, languid fragrance of jessamine and nightscented stock drifting in through the open windows. Tim put an arm around my shoulders and gently caressed the nape of my neck. Presently he drew me into a close embrace and I let him kiss me. I longed for the magic to work again as it had the other night. I longed for all my suspicions to be washed away in a wave of emotion.

But this evening the magic was lacking. After a while Tim drew back.

'What's wrong, Tracy?'

'Nothing. Oh, I don't know...'

'There is something,' he insisted, an edge to his voice. 'But you refuse to say what it is. Right?'

I shook my head silently, non-committally. Tim looked at me long and hard, and I dreaded that he was going to nail me down into telling him. If I were forced to admit that—my mind at war with my heart—I thought he might possibly be the writer of a poisonous letter about me; that he might be responsible for something infinitely more dreadful....what then?

I shuddered, and made myself speak in a

calm, reasonable voice.

'Tim...I'm just rather tired. I suppose all this business over Oliver, and...and Ursula being killed, too...it's just upset me more than I imagined.'

'Are you sure that's all it is?' he asked doubtfully.

'Yes, of course. What else could it be? Perhaps you'd better go now.'

Tim needed a lot of persuading. He argued that it was better for me to have his company than to work myself into an even moodier state on my own. But he left in the end, saying that he'd ring me in the morning, first thing, to see how I was feeling by then.

I went to bed at once, deeply depressed. How was it possible to love a man if you could ten per-cent—even a half of one per-cent—believe him capable of committing the most unspeakable crime?

I had no answer to that. I only knew, as I lay wide-eyed and sleepless in the big Victorian brass-knobbed bed which had been my aunt's, that I wished I hadn't sent Tim home.

In the end I slept heavily. The phone woke me from an unpleasant dream of shapeless fears. Squinting at the pendulum clock on the landing as I ran past it down to the hall, I saw

208

that it was not yet seven-thirty. The sound of Tim's voice immediately banished sleepiness.

'Sorry if I woke you, Tracy. You see, it struck me in the middle of the night that I'd left you stranded without your car. It's still at the studio.'

'Oh yes! I hadn't given that a thought.'

'I'll come and pick you up. Just tell me what time.'

'There's no need,' I protested. 'I can easily walk.'

'No, I'll come. Nine o'clock? A quarter to, or a quarter past? Just say.'

'Well, nine o'clock, then. Thanks for thinking of it.'

It was absurd, this confusion about Tim. I felt resentful towards Neil, as if the possibility of Tim's guilt had come about through his suspicions, and not the other way round.

When Tim arrived I was ready and waiting at the front door, to allow him no excuse for coming in. On the way to the studio he asked me how I was feeling, and I gave him an evasive answer. There was tension between us and I was thankful that it was only a short drive.

'Do I see you this evening, Tracy?' he asked, as I went to get out.

I improvised hastily, 'I'll be hellishly busy, I've got so far behind. I was thinking of putting in some extra time here.'

'But you can't go on working all evening,' Tim protested.

'You did the other night,' I pointed out. 'Until after midnight, you said.'

He gave me an odd look. 'That was different, my VAT return had to be done at once.'

'So must my work. If I'm going to make any sort of name for myself, I can't afford to let my clients feel neglected.'

His look changed to one of anger. 'Why not come straight out and just say you don't want to see me?'

'Is that what you'd prefer me to say?' I retorted.

It was almost frightening, the way we could so quickly plunge towards a quarrel. But whatever Tim might have answered he was prevented by the sound of approaching footsteps. We both swung round and saw Sir Robert Medway coming through the archway. Using his arrival as an excuse to break it up with Tim, I jumped out of the car.

'Good morning, Sir Robert.'

'Ah, Miss Yorke, good morning. I'm glad to have caught you, I wanted a word. If you are free, that is...'

Tim, half out of the car too, put in hastily, 'It's all right, Sir Robert, I was just leaving.'

To me, he said, 'See you, Tracy.'

I unlocked the door and led the way upstairs, Sir Robert pausing halfway to regain his breath. In the studio he accepted the chair I pulled forward for him and sank down into it gratefully. For a while he sat getting a grip on himself, his two hands resting on the bone handle of the cane he held between his knees. He looked no better than at Oliver's funeral yesterday, his bloodless skin stretched tight, his eyes tormented.

'Do you see much of that young man, Miss Yorke?' he asked in a thin, cracked sort of voice.

'I've seen a fair bit of him lately,' I admitted.

'I didn't realise that there was anything between you two.'

'There isn't really,' I said quickly, then added in a less defensive tone, 'Tim and I have known each other since we were quite young. He kindly called for me this morning because he happened to know that I'd left my car here last night.'

'I see,' said Sir Robert, nodding his head. 'An accquaintance of long standing. I expect there are a number of people in and around Steeple Haslop with whom you are on such terms?'

'Well, yes, I do know quite a number of people.'

The bony jaw worked as if he were chewing over some invisible problem.

'You must miss my son, Miss Yorke,' he said, after a moment.

'I do, Sir Robert. I looked upon Oliver as a very good friend.'

'You and he talked a great deal, I expect?'

'Yes, we did.'

'And not just about business matters?'

'We chatted about all sorts of things,' I said, wondering where this was leading. 'Oliver liked to talk, as you well know, and I always found what he had to say very interesting.' This was putting it as kindly as I could. There had been times when I'd longed to tell Oliver to shut up and let me get on with my work.

Sir Robert had laid aside his walking stick and now sat with his hands in his lap. Both fists were clenched into tight balls, I noticed. There was a very long pause, while he made a business of clearing his throat.

'I have been giving much thought to this matter,' he said at last. 'As long as you remain here...in Steeple Haslop, I mean, but particularly in this studio, there is so much to remind you...'

'That's true, of course. At first I wondered

212

if I'd ever be able to face working in this room, but I knew that I'd have to clear up the current work, and gradually I've come to terms with it.'

'But it cannot be easy. Now hear what I have to say, Miss Yorke. You are young, my dear. Would it not be better to cut loose and make a new beginning elsewhere?'

'Elsewhere?'

'In London, perhaps. The opportunities there must be considerably greater than in a small village.'

I felt a spurt of anger. Sir Robert's approach had been a roundabout one, but his objective was now suddenly obvious. It occurred to me to wonder if Sebastian was behind the manoeuvre.

'Does this mean that you are withdrawing the offer you made the other day?' I asked frostily.

'Not at all, Miss Yorke.' He looked distressed at the suggestion. 'You mustn't think anything of the kind. My only concern is whether I have been sufficiently generous.'

'Then I don't understand what you are getting at, Sir Robert.'

'Simply this, my dear child—that our little ...arrangement need not be contingent upon you carrying on at the studio here. If you prefer the wider scope that London offers, why not go there?'

I almost gaped at him in astonishment. 'You mean that if I choose to set up business in London, I could still look to you for financial help?'

'Indeed, yes! Do you like the idea, Miss Yorke?'

I didn't like it one bit. The thought of leaving Steeple Haslop now, of leaving Tim, was so unattractive as to be out of the question. Which indicated, though I didn't work it out at that moment, what little credence I put in the theory that Tim might be guilty of murder.

'I would prefer to leave matters as we have already agreed, Sir Robert,' I said decisively.

He looked nonplussed. 'But surely...you told me yourself that you might find it difficult to run a successful business here without Oliver's contacts.'

'That would apply with even greater force in London,' I pointed out. 'At least, around here, I have gained a certain reputation through my association with Oliver. In London I'd have to start from scratch.'

Sir Robert fixed his gaze on the ceramic mural of abstract leaf patterns, as if seeking inspiration from it.

'Doubtless,' he said, 'I could give you a few introductions to possible clients from among my acquaintances. And you wouldn't need to concern yourself too much about making a profit, Miss Yorke. I could see to it that you were able to draw at least the same salary that you have been receiving here.'

I looked at him squarely. 'Sir Robert, I was—and am—grateful to you for your offer to let me take over the Design Studio, and give me financial backing. I intend to work hard at it. I intend to be able to repay you eventually and, I hope, even show you a small profit. But no way is that likely in London, not in the foreseeable future.'

Sir Robert Medway looked bewildered—more than that, a little desperate.

'Is it because of your cottage that you are hesitating? I could make you a good offer for that. Considerably above the market value. And as for an income...well, I recognise that it is more expensive living in London, and I wouldn't want to stint you.'

'Sir Robert, I just don't want to leave Steeple Haslop.'

'If it is still a question of money, then...'

'It has nothing to do with money,' I declared. 'If you were to withdraw your offer completely, I would still stay on in Steeple Haslop. I've decided that now. Somehow or other I'd find a way to manage.'

Sir Robert leant forward in his chair, clutching at the stainless-steel edge of my table to support himself. He stared at me wildly.

'Why are you so insistent about staying here, Miss Yorke? What precisely is your motive?'

'Motive? It's more a matter of inclination. I like it here. I feel that I belong here. I have friends here...'

'You must have made friends when you were in London.'

'I did, but that was different. They were mostly the sort of people who will have moved on to other places by now. Whereas most of the people around here I've known since I was a child. It's a feeling of having roots, I suppose.' I was waffling, wrapping up the real reason why I wanted to stay on here—Tim Baxter. Not that I had any need to justify myself to Sir Robert, I thought angrily, so why did I feel my cheeks burning with colour?

'I see.' He looked really at a loss now. I had a feeling that I'd only to drop the tiniest hint to have him offer me yet more money. To forestall that, I asked, 'Why are you so anxious for me to leave, Sir Robert?'

'I am considering your interests, and yours alone. I am trying to assist in forwarding your future, that is all.'

We looked at one another. There seemed to be nothing more to be said. But then Sir Robert coughed, and began hesitantly, 'I want you to give me your promise, Miss Yorke.'

'My promise?'

'I want you to remember that you can always call on me if you are in any kind of difficulty—financial or otherwise. Problems are always best kept within the family, I am sure you will agree. And considering your close association with Oliver, we think of you almost as one of the family, my wife and I. So I want you to promise me that if anything crops up, I shall be the person to whom you will turn, and no one else.'

He looked so agitated, so distressed, that I gave him the promise he wanted. It seemed to bring him a small degree of satisfaction, and some of the tension went out of him.

'And how are you for money at the moment, my dear child? Is it difficult for you, with the studio's bank account frozen for the time being?'

'Not really. None of the bills are overdue for payment, and I'm fine personally.'

Sir Robert nodded his head slowly. 'But you will let me know if you run short? I am a wealthy man, and it would be the easiest thing in the world for me to relieve you of any financial anxiety.'

'It's very kind of you, Sir Robert,' I murmured, much embarrassed.

'Not at all, not at all!' He seemed to drift off into a daydream, then pulled himself up sharply. 'I had better be going. I'm preventing you from working.'

I followed close behind as he descended the stairs, ready to grab hold of him if he stumbled. But he made it unaided. As I watched him stride off uncertainly across the courtyard, my mind was busy with speculation about the reasons behind his visit.

CHAPTER 12

'Could it be,' suggested Neil lightly, 'that he fancies the idea of having an attractive young protégé set up in London?'

'If you're going to make silly jokes,' I said, 'I wish I hadn't told you.'

Neil's smile vanished. 'I'm glad you did, though. This could be important.'

I had spent most of the morning since Sir Robert's departure debating what I ought to do. Was his strange attitude something Neil should know about, or was I just being stupid? It could be that Sir Robert's intention, his only intention, was to compensate me for being left in an awkward situation by Oliver's death. And perhaps he had become so upset at my refusal to go along with his plans merely because he was an autocrat who didn't care for the recipients of his patronage having minds of their own.

Perhaps...but I couldn't persuade myself to believe that.

Neil had resolved my doubts about what to do by walking in on me soon after noon, inviting me to have lunch with him. He sensed at once that something was bugging me, and it didn't take him long to dig out what it was.

'What's the explanation?' I demanded, when Neil had made me go through the conversation with Sir Robert as nearly word for word as I could remember it. I wanted him to come up with a simple answer.

'One thing's certain,' he mused. 'Despite Sir Robert's claim to the contrary, he's very determined to get you out of the way. Somehow your presence represents a danger to him, or to his family. This suggests there's something you know—or something he *thinks* you know, or might come to know.'

'Yes, but what? Of course, there's that business about Sebastian being in the neighbourhood on the morning Oliver was killed.'

Neil shook his head. 'I can't believe it's that. When I talked to Sebastian he seemed extremely anxious to conceal the fact from his father. So if for some reason he later felt compelled to make a clean breast of it, then presumably Sir Robert is fully aware that the police already have the information.' Neil ledged himself on the back of a chair. 'My hunch is that it's something to do with Lady Medway. How much do you know about her and Oliver?'

'Lady Medway and Oliver? You don't mean,

for heaven's sake, that you think there was anything between them?'

'It can't be ruled out.' He gave me a direct look. 'Weren't you aware that Sir Robert and his wife first met one another through Oliver?'

'Honestly? I had no idea.'

'Maybe Sir Robert is under the impression that Oliver told you more than he in fact did.' After a brief pause, Neil went on. 'This must be for your private ear alone, Tracy. Investigations concerning Oliver Medway that we've had made in London suggest that he and Diana Chivers—as Lady Medway was in those days—were a good deal more than friends.'

'Come off it, Neil,' I protested. 'You aren't going to make me believe that Sir Robert is the sort of man to accept his own son's cast-offs.'

'Not knowingly. I doubt if Sir Robert had the faintest glimmer of what there was between those two. Diana, it appears, saw the father as the better prospect. She was approaching the age when parts are harder to find, and she probably realised that she'd never get a proposal of marriage out of Oliver. Then after she and the old boy were happily spliced, Oliver returned here to live. A very cosy and convenient little arrangement, if he had a fancy to pick up again with Diana. And from what I know about Oliver Medway's character, it would have amused him to carry on with his father's wife right under the parental nose.'

I challenged Neil with a glare. 'Have you got the slightest evidence that this was happening?'

'Nothing definite. Our chaps have picked up one or two hints, though...straws in the wind, you might say.'

'I would have known about it,' I objected. 'I'm sure I would have known if there was anything between them.'

'Would you, Tracy?' He allowed the question to linger, then said, 'You like to think that you knew the man pretty well, but just consider. There was clearly more between Medway and Mrs Kemp than you were aware of—whatever the exact nature of their relationship. So he'd probably have been even more careful to conceal from you any goings-on with his stepmother.'

'I suppose so,' I allowed grudgingly.

These past few days I'd had so many surprises about Oliver that I no longer felt able to trust my instincts where he was concerned.

'But if Oliver was so careful to keep their relationship secret,' I argued, 'then his *father* wouldn't have been likely to know about it, either...Are you suggesting that Sir Robert has found out about it since?'

Neil shook his head. 'It's more likely—if we

really are on the right track—that he found out just before his son's death. Remember that Sir Robert and Lady Medway had the very dickens of a row earlier that same morning.'

A sudden excitement took hold of me. Desperate for a solution that would absolve Tim, I was ready to grasp at any wild theory.

'You're not suggesting, Neil, that Sir Robert was so enraged that he killed his own son.'

'Possibly. It's also possible that it was Lady Medway who killed Oliver in a jealous quarrel. Either way, Sir Robert would be frantic for his son's murder to remain unsolved. But as long as you're around, Tracy, you represent a threat.'

'How could I be a threat to him?'

'Could be, as I said, that he thinks Oliver told you more than he actually did. And that sooner or later you'll be putting two and two together, even if you haven't got around to it yet. When talking about Oliver to me, for instance, or other people for that matter, some forgotten fragment of knowledge might suddenly snap back into place and become significant. So, Sir Robert wants you safely out of the way—and nicely indebted to him into the bargain, so that you'll never be tempted to talk out of turn.'

Sir Robert *had* close-questioned me about

how much Oliver and I had talked together. And not only had Sir Robert pressed money upon me, he'd also been insistent that he was the first person I should consider turning to if faced with any sort of financial problem. Was it his veiled way of offering a bribe for my silence?

'But if your theory is true,' I reasoned, 'then why did Sir Robert originally suggest an arrangement that would actually have *prevented* my leaving Steeple Haslop?'

Neil gave me a rueful grin. 'That's the trouble with theories. They carry you just so far, but there's always a weak point somewhere.'

'And how does Ursula fit into all this?' I threw at him. But instead of flooring Neil completely, the question seemed to perk him up a bit.

'We've already agreed, haven't we, that there was a special closeness between Ursula Kemp and Oliver Medway. Just suppose that he really was having an affair with his stepmother, wouldn't he have found it almost unendurable not to be able to share the joke with *some*one?'

'You mean, he told Ursula about it?'

'He might have thought she was the one person it was safe to confide in. Perhaps Mrs Kemp felt a twisted sort of maternal pride in Oliver.'

I thought a moment, and was forced to admit it was possible. Ursula Kemp had been an enigma, without friends or any apparent interest in Steeple Haslop's social life.

I looked at Neil. 'You think, then, that Sir Robert somehow found out that Ursula knew about it?'

'Might she have tried to blackmail him, Tracy?'

'And Sir Robert killed her?'

'He, or his wife,' said Neil. 'Or both of them together.'

'No, I don't think that's at all likely,' I said firmly. 'They don't seem at all close, those two. It's something I've noticed particularly each time I've seen them together since Oliver's death. Here in the flat that first morning, then at the inquest. And again yesterday during the funeral service and afterwards at the house.'

'But that could even add weight to my argument. If one—or both—of them were responsible for the deaths of Oliver and Mrs Kemp, then there would inevitably be an estrangement between them, considering the motive for the murders. Yet, however far apart the Medways might feel, they'd be chained together forever by their guilt. Chained by mutual hatred. Chained by fear. They'd each be as anxious as the other one to prevent the truth from coming to light, so they might well co-operate in taking whatever steps seem necessary.'

'It's possible, I suppose,' I said, with a shiver.

'The history of murder is littered with cases which prove that point.' Neil pushed himself away from the chairback and started pacing restlessly around the studio. 'It could be worth having another go at our young friend Sebastian.'

'You mean Sebastian might be in it with them?'

'I shouldn't think so.' Neil hesitated in the way I'd come to recognise. He was, I felt sure, considering how much he should tell me. Then he continued, 'For all practical purposes, we've eliminated Sebastian Medway from suspicion. The explanation for his presence hereabouts last Wednesday morning checks out. Although he cannot account for every single minute of his time so as to make it out of the question that he killed his stepbrother, it would need to have been with the woman's connivance. And I somehow don't think that's likely.'

'The woman?'

'You already knew that he was with a woman. Grace Ebborn saw them together in the Volvo, remember?'

'Yes, of course. But the way you said it, Neil,

seemed to imply that she and Sebastain were... well, having it off.'

He turned his head and grinned. 'Those two were making a late start returning to Oxford, after spending a night at her cottage over Little Edgecombe way.'

That really did surprise me. 'But, I mean... Sebastian isn't the sort to...'

Did I detect reluctant admiration in Neil's broadening grin?'

'You've been fooled, Tracy, by the image he was so anxious to present to his adoptive daddy as a reassuring contrast to Oliver's screwing around. But from the enquiries we've made in Oxford, young Sebastian is quite a lad, too— in his own very discreet way. About his latest exploit, he informed us himself—he had to, in order to clinch his alibi. He really is playing with fireworks this time, because the woman happens to be the wife of his professor. It would make quite a scandal at the university if it came to light, and some of the stray sparks might well reach Sir Robert.'

'And do I take it that it's now your intention to use what you know about Sebastian as a threat, in the hope of bulldozing him into making some sort of revelation about his father and stepmother?'

'It will be done with finesse, of course. Kid

gloves for the Medways, remember—them's my orders.'

I threw a sour look at Neil's back as he continued prowling.

'I'm beginning to learn something about your kid gloves. You use them on everyone, don't you? Get them talking, let drop a few trivial scraps of information to make them feel that you're taking them into your confidence...as I suppose you planned to do with Ursula. And I'm perfectly well aware that it's what you're doing with me.'

He turned on me reproachfully. 'With you I've done one hell of a lot more than let drop a few trivial scraps of information.'

'But you still haven't told me a single word more than you intended me to know, have you?'

'Would you expect me to? I'm a policeman, remember.'

'Yes, a policeman first, last, and all the time!'

He came nearer and gave me a long, steady look.

'Not *all* the time, Tracy,' he said softly. 'And to prove my point, let's go out to lunch and find something else to talk about.'

'Such as what?' I demanded suspiciously.

'Use your imagination. If we try very hard, I'll bet we can think of something.'

We went to the Trout Inn again. Today, sitting opposite one another at a table on the trellised patio, we tried their Cotswold lamb cutlets with glazed carrots and fresh green peas. Neil flirted with me the entire time....lightly, brightly, and wittily.

When Neil drove me back to the studio I was expecting him to continue on to Haslop Hall to interview Sebastian. But as I settled to work, I realised that I hadn't heard his car start up. So I went through to the flat where I could look down into the courtyard. Neil was still there, talking to Billy Moon. Coming at it pretty heavy, too, judging from the way the old chap's shoulders were hunched.

What was he intent on finding out now? The comings and goings up to the Coach House flat? Billy kept all sorts of odd hours, preferring the company of his horses to going to the pub or watching television in his cottage. Sometimes he'd be in the stable area quite late in the evening, pottering around, or just sitting smoking his pipe. He had been known to spend the whole night there when a horse seemed a bit sickly.

Might he have spotted Lady Medway slipping in for a secret assignation with Oliver? If so, I wondered if anything would ever persuade

229

him to disclose the fact. Billy mistrusted people; he talked to his horses, I suspected, far more than he had ever talked to a fellow human being.

Neil appeared to be delivering a lecture to Billy, one finger raised for emphasis. Then, as I watched, he strode to his car, got in and drove swiftly away.

Poor Billy looked so crushed that I felt an urge to try and cheer him up. I remembered that I hadn't kept my promise to him. Returning to the studio, I unearthed the June issue of *Cotswold Illustrated* from beneath some sample boards I'd been looking at earlier. I tore off the cover and trimmed the photograph with scissors as Billy had done.

I found the old man in the tack room, sitting perched at his high desk staring morosely into space.

'Billy, I almost forgot. Here's the picture I promised you as a replacement.'

I laid it down in front of him on the sloping desk top, and he glanced at it without interest.

'Aye, miss.'

'Aren't you feeling well?' I ventured. 'You don't look too good.'

'I'm all right!' Then after a moment, he burst out, 'Them coppers, they're s'posed to be catching criminals. They ought to leave honest folks to theirselves.'

'But if a serious crime has been committed,' I pointed out gently, 'the only way the police can ever arrive at the truth is to piece together lots of bits of information from different people. And to do that they have to ask lots of questions.'

'Well, they can't get nothing from me,' he growled, ''cause I don't know nothing. Like I keeps telling 'em.'

'But you see,' I said patiently, 'you might know something important without even realising it yourself. I mean, something you saw or heard that you hardly took any notice of at the time.'

'Aye,' he said, 'and before you knows where you are they'd have you standing up in court as a witness or something. No good never came of that sort of thing.'

'But it's your *duty* to tell the police anything you know,' I said earnestly, feeling like a preacher. 'Your public duty.'

Billy shook his head stubbornly. 'I keeps meself to meself, miss...I always have and I always will. Besides,' he mumbled, 'I don't know nothing, so there.'

But he did know something; I suddenly felt convinced of it.

'Think about it, Billy,' I begged him. 'The

231

awful thing about murder is that the killer often strikes again if he's not caught. You might be the one and only person who can solve this case. I'm sure you wouldn't want it on your conscience if somebody else was murdered, too.'

CHAPTER 13

The phone began to ring as I walked back to the studio, and I ran upstairs thinking—hoping—that it would be Tim. Instead, it was a case of panic stations. At Myddleton Manor, the contractor was having a problem with the kitchen fitments. Somewhere in my drawings there was a discrepancy of ten millimetres, and according to him it was throwing everything off.

I drove over there at once, and quickly discovered the source of the error. The plasterer had rendered the walls precisely to my scale, not allowing for the thickness of the glazed tiles that were fixed afterwards. With the conversion already running behind schedule, and the owners due back from their holiday in less than a week, I had to make some rapid adjustments.

By the time I was through, I had half a mind to pack it in for the day and go straight home. What was the point of pushing ahead with the work when everything might easily collapse around my ears? The way things were developing, Sir Robert's grace and favour might prove to be worth less than nothing to me.

But a defeatist attitude, I told myself sternly, was no way to run a successful business enterprise. Better to keep plodding on. Besides —and the thought made me speed a little faster back to the studio—I had told Tim that I'd be working late this evening. If he did ring or call around and found me not there, I'd be caught out in a flat lie. I'd hate that to happen.

I longed for Tim to call so I could say I was sorry. But why I was sorry, there was no way I could explain to him. How could I possibly admit to Tim that I'd imagined him capable of murder? And the fact that I no longer suspected him was without logic, merely because Neil was off on a new line of enquiry. But Neil had all along had various possibilities in mind—including myself in the role of Oliver's murderer. Nothing had really changed.

I sat down and started writing letters to architects and builders in the county who might be in a position to put work my way, explaining that I was continuing the Design Studio on my own. The job was boringly repetitive, but at least it had the merit of not calling for much mental effort. It began to grow dark and I put the lights on, still plugging away at the typewriter. I would just finish this one, I promised myself, then I'd call a halt.

The sound of a car turning in through the archway made me pause and listen. My heartbeat quickened. It was Tim's car, surely? I had locked the outer door, and I ran downstairs to open it.

'Hallo, Tracy. Still slogging away?'

'I was just finishing, actually.'

He smiled his lopsided smile. 'I timed it just right, didn't I? Let's go and eat somewhere.'

'Oh...yes, if you like.' Though I'd been longing for Tim to get in touch with me, now that he was here I felt oddly shy. I injected a little more enthusiasm into my voice. 'That would be super.'

Warily, as if half-expecting a brush-off, he came forward and slid his arms around me.

'You're a strange girl, Tracy. I know that some women turn on and off to keep a chap guessing, but...'

'I'm not playing games, Tim.'

'No,' he said gravely, 'that's exactly what I mean. With you there's more to it. So why not tell me?'

'There's nothing to tell.'

For a moment he just held me, and there was a puzzled pained look in his eyes. Then swiftly he bent his head and found my lips. I clung to him, melting against his lean body.

As he let me go, he said, 'But you really must

come clean. There's something that's badly bothering you, and I expect to be told what it is.'

It was like an icy blast on a summer's day. I shivered, and drew back from him. Then I said in an even tone, 'Why does it surprise you that I'm knocked a bit sideways just now? It was a terrific shock, finding Oliver dead like that. I daresay that it'll be quite some time before I really get over it.'

'Is that honestly all that's been making you so tense?'

'Isn't it enough? And then there's Ursula, too.'

'Ursula?' he questioned, with a quick frown. 'Oliver I can understand—just about—but Ursula Kemp was no more than an acquaintance. Lots of people get killed in road accidents. You've no more reason to be upset over her than anyone else, have you?'

'I suppose not, but...'

'But nothing!' There was a bite in his voice as he went on, 'I'm trying to help you snap out of this mood, Tracy. Whatever it is you've got on your mind, you'd better tell me about it.'

'There isn't anything,' I said desperately. 'I'm just feeling a bit low, that's all.'

Tim started to object again, but the phone rang.

'Who would that be?' he asked, annoyed at the interruption.

'I've no idea.' I scooped up the phone and gave my number.

'Tracy!' It was Neil's voice. 'What a relief to have caught you. I tried to reach you at home, and when I couldn't I was a bit anxious.'

'Anxious, Neil?'

'Damned worried, in fact. I take it that you're alone at the moment?'

'Er...yes,' I said, without quite understanding why. 'What's the problem?'

'Look, I know this will seem strange to you, but I want you to promise me something. If Tim Baxter gets in touch with you in the next half hour or so and wants you to meet him—don't. And don't let him in if he calls round.'

I stole a glance at Tim. He looked puzzled, but clearly hadn't heard Neil's actual words. Pressing the phone closer to my ear, I said, 'What's all this about, Neil?'

'I'll explain later.'

'No, now,' I insisted. 'I want to know.'

He gave an exasperated sigh. 'All right, but I haven't much time. So don't ask questions, and don't argue. I've just had that old chap Billy Moon down at the station...'

'Billy Moon? But what's he got to do with...?'

'I decided that Billy knew more than he was telling and that I'd have to squeeze it out of him. And then, when I got him here, he started talking without any trouble at all...said he'd already decided that he should. Apparently it was you who made him see sense.'

'What did he tell you?' I asked nervously.

'Something very interesting—that Tim Baxter had visited the studio on the morning Oliver Medway was killed. Earlier, that is, than when he burst in on you. To be precise, at eleven-thirty. It seems that Baxter arrived in the courtyard on foot, which was odd in itself, and Billy happened to spot him through the window of the tack room. He didn't think anything of it, though. But a few minutes later he was passing the studio stairs carrying a bucket and he heard raised voices coming from above. He couldn't make out what it was all about, but he said that Medway and Baxter were really shouting at each other.'

I was too shocked to speak. Each pulse seemed to thud in my ears like the beat of a drum.

'Are you still there, Tracy?'

'Yes,' I whispered hoarsely. 'I'm here.'

Glancing up, I met Tim's eyes and looked away quickly. How much had he deciphered of this? Had he guessed what was being said ...from the tone of Neil's voice, from my own curious responses? But there was no hint of understanding in his expression, only puzzlement. I clamped the phone even closer to my ear as Neil went on speaking.

'It looks very black for Baxter,' he was saying. 'I've always been suspicious of the reason he gave me for visiting the studio that morning, and that business about wiping your prints off the statuette took a lot of swallowing, too. Besides he was seen coming away from Ursula Kemp's place on Sunday, after dark.'

'You...you didn't tell me that,' I stammered.

'I didn't tell you everthing, Tracy—especially about Baxter, knowing that you were seeing so much of him. A police car is on its way to the vineyard to pick Baxter up right now. So if he happens to phone you, for God's sake watch what you say. He mustn't get the slightest hint that we're on to him. Okay?'

'But Neil...'

'Leave it, Tracy. I'm up to my eyes, and I've spent far too much time talking to you already. I'll be in touch again just as soon as I can. Bye for now.'

There was a click, and I was left with the dialling tone. Putting down the phone seemed like cutting the lifeline to safety. Here in the studio I was a long way from any kind of help. The nearest people were at the Hall, far beyond shouting distance. The Medways...they were in the clear now, of course, all three of them.

Certainty of Tim's guilt came crashing down, paralysing me with misery and fear. Everything fitted so neatly. I had been correct in my first instinctive thought that the retreating footsteps I'd heard that morning were Tim's, and that he had returned to the studio a few minutes later to finish what my arrival had interrupted ...the removal of tell-tale evidence, like his fingerprints on the murder weapon.

And there was something else, too, a little scrap of knowledge that had been lying dormant in my mind. I groped for it now, but couldn't bring it to the surface, though awareness of something deeply significant prodded at me.

Tim was standing watching me, impatiently twirling his key ring on his little finger, the key ring which carried the chased-silver medallion.

An image suddenly zoomed into focus, the scene in the studio when I'd come in to find Oliver's body. On the hexagonal desk, the morning's mail had been opened and strewn across it in Oliver's usual careless manner; there was the white telephone, an auction catalogue he'd been studying...and a bunch of keys. Things so normal that they'd hardly registered—except that at the time I hadn't recognised that bunch of keys.

I felt sick in my stomach. The keys I'd seen on Oliver's desk had been the same bunch Tim was holding now. No wonder the good-luck charm had struck me as familiar when I'd been looking at it in the pub yesterday. He must have had them in his hand the way he so often did, as he had now, and dropped them on the desk as he'd reached for the statuette. An absolutely damning piece of evidence if the police had found those keys at the scene of the crime.

Tim had been forced to take the risk of returning to the studio, not only to remove his fingerprints from the statuette, but to stealthily pocket his key ring.

When Tim spoke there seemed to be menace in his voice.

'That was a peculiar conversation you just had with Neil Grant. What was he phoning you about?'

Feeling desperate, I wondered how to keep Tim off the scent. What could I say that would satisfy his curiosity?

'You said something about Billy Moon,' he prompted.

'Did I? Oh yes, that was just...just about what a stubborn old cuss Billy can be. They wanted a statement from him, and he wouldn't co-operate.'

'Why should they want a statement from Billy Moon?'

'Why? Well, I suppose...because he happens to work in the stables they thought that he might...' I trailed off. Every syllable seemed to be heading me closer to a dangerous admission.

Tim's brown eyes narrowed. 'They think he might have seen something, you mean?'

'It's...it's possible, I suppose.'

'And why the devil should Neil Grant phone to tell you about that?' he demanded. 'Just what's going on between you two?'

'Nothing! Neil just happened to mention it, that's all.'

Without warning Tim's hand shot out and his fingers clamped tightly on my wrist.

'That damn chap is always hanging round you—popping in to see you here and at home, taking you out to lunch. I want to know what the hell you're playing at.'

Stupid with fear, I tried to make myself *think*. I had to find an explanation that Tim would find plausible. The best way was to make out that Neil's interest in me was purely personal, nothing to do with the police investigation at all.

'It's just that Neil fancies me a bit,' I said with a shrug, forcing myself not to pull my hand away from Tim. 'I've realised it for several days now—not that I've given him the least encouragement.'

'Haven't you?'

'No, I haven't! I suppose that's why he keeps telling me bits and pieces about the murder enquiry, to try and get me interested in him.'

'It seems to me that Grant tells you every bloody little detail of his working day! All that chatting away on the phone just now.'

I threw in a flat lie to add conviction to my story. 'Well...Neil was trying to make a date with me.'

'It didn't sound like that. And if it was, you didn't exactly slap him down, Tracy.'

'I...I don't need to slap him down,' I stammered. 'He'll get the message in the end, don't worry about that.' Before Tim could say anything more, I rushed on, 'Look, I'm absolutely starving. Let's go back to Honeysuckle Cottage and I'll knock up a meal for us.'

He hesitated. 'All right, then.'

'Okay, I won't be a minute. I must just slip along to the bathroom.'

Gathering up my handbag, I went through the communicating door to the flat. In case Tim was listening, I popped in the bathroom first and turned on the basin taps, leaving them running. Then, very quietly, in a fever of caution,

I crept down the flat's staircase, letting myself out into the courtyard. I didn't close the front door behind me, in case Tim might hear the click.

He would hear the car's engine, of course, but by then I'd have a good start. Once he realised that I was running out on him, he'd soon guess why. I had to get to people...anyone would do.

My first thought as I started the engine was to make for the Hall. But once through the archway, I turned left along the main drive out of the grounds. The Hall was too near and Tim might have caught up with me in the time it took Grainger to don his black butler's jacket and make his stately progress to the door.

I glanced in the rear view mirror. There were no headlights as yet. If I could only reach the village, there'd be somebody around. I could pull up at the Trout Inn and dive into the bar. There, among people, I'd be safe. And all I'd have to do was get in touch with Neil.

Turning out of the entrance gates, I drove fast down the hill and into the village. There were lights on behind curtained windows, but the street itself seemed deserted. Then ahead of me I saw a man's figure. It was Ralph Ebborn, just emerging from the front gate of The Larches. I screeched to a stop beside him.

Ralph looked surprised, and not in the least pleased to see me. But our disagreement would have to be forgotten now.

'What in heaven's name is the matter, Tracy?' he asked, as I leapt out of the car. 'You must have been doing sixty.'

'Ralph, I...' At first, spotting him, I'd known only relief. Now it came through to me that I had a lot of explaining to do, and it wasn't going to be easy. 'I must talk to you,' I finished.

'I was just going to the Trout for a drink,' he said, with an indifferent shrug. 'What is it?'

'Can't we go into the house, Ralph? I'd feel happier there.'

'Grace isn't home. She's gone to Stratford with a Women's Institute party to see *Othello*.'

'It doesn't matter.'

He regarded me doubtfully, then nodded. 'Okay, come in and tell me what's on your mind.'

Inside the hallway, I said, 'Can I use the phone first?'

'Who do you want to ring?'

'The police. Or rather, Neil Grant.'

Ralph turned his head and looked at me. 'What d'you want to talk to him for? There's not been an accident or anything like that, has there?'

'Oh no. But I have some information I must pass on to him.' I gave a shudder. 'I don't like having to do it,' I admitted with a sigh. 'But I suppose I've got to.'

Ralph threw open the door of the sitting room. Switching on the lights, he gestured me inside.

'Why not come on in and tell me about it first,' he said, in a more friendly tone. 'Then we can decide what's best to be done.'

'But Ralph...'

'You look in a real dither, Tracy. Sit down and I'll get you a drink. You obviously need one.'

'Yes, I do rather.'

A few sips of brandy helped to dull the pain a little and, shakily, I began to put Ralph in the picture. He listened in sheer astonishment.

'You mean to tell me,' he broke in, 'that old Billy Moon actually saw Baxter go up to the studio that morning, and overheard him having a row with Oliver?' He scratched his chin thoughtfully. 'Why has Billy only just got around to telling the police about it?'

'You know what Billy can be like, stubborn as a mule. But then he suddenly realised that it was wrong to conceal such a vital piece of information.'

'That's all the police have managed to get out

of him, though?'

'Isn't it enough?' I said wretchedly. 'Especially now it's emerged that Tim was seen visiting Ursula Kemp the other night, after dark.'

'Ursula Kemp?' echoed Ralph, looking very puzzled. 'How does she come into it?'

'I'll explain in a minute,' I said, realising what a mess I was making of my story. I went on, deeply unhappy, 'To be honest, Ralph, I was suspicious of Tim right at the start...I mean, the way he appeared on the scene immediately after I arrived at the studio and found Oliver's body. And then when he wiped the fingerprints off the statuette...'

'He did what?'

'I was holding it, you see, when I heard someone coming...I'd picked the thing up instinctively. So Tim wiped it clean, saying that it would complicate things if the police found *my* prints on the murder weapon. But I thought at the time that he could easily be wiping off his own fingerprints as well.'

'Good God! Do the police know about that little episode?'

'Yes, they do. Neil gave us both a real dressing down. But there was nothing else to implicate Tim Baxter—not at the time. If only the business of the keys had struck me then.'

'Keys? What keys, Tracy?'

'Tim's key ring was on Oliver's desk when I got to the studio that morning. It just didn't strike me at the time, and of course at that stage I wouldn't have known whose they were anyway. Tim has a curious little medallion attached to the ring, you see, and when I happened to notice it yesterday, he explained to me that it had been hand made at a street market in France. Somehow it seemed familiar, but I didn't realise *why* until just now, back at the studio, when Tim had his keys dangling from his finger. It suddenly brought back a vivid recollection of Oliver's desk that day, with the bunch of keys lying on it. That's what Tim must have come back for—that and to wipe his fingerprints off the statuette—and, of course, he had plenty of opportunity to pocket the keys while I was away fetching Sir Robert.'

Ralph frowned. 'Does Baxter realise that you know all this, Tracy?'

'Well, I didn't actually say anything. I was careful not to. But Tim must have guessed, from the way I ran out on him. I fully expected him to come chasing after me, but he doesn't seem to have done.'

'No,' said Ralph, looking thoughtful, 'he doesn't.'

'I suppose I ought to phone Neil Grant now

and tell him what's happened,' I said reluctantly.

'That can wait,' said Ralph, with a shake of his head. 'Finish telling me about it, first. What made the police concentrate on Billy Moon?'

'Neil always had a feeling that Billy knew more than he'd admit to. And then there was the matter of his finding the magazine.'

'Magazine?' Ralph looked mystified. 'You haven't mentioned that before.'

'Oh, haven't I? I'm afraid I'm not thinking very clearly. You see, Billy found a copy of *Cotswold Illustrated* stuffed down behind the manger in the stables, and it was obviously the one used to make up that anonymous letter about me...' I saw a fresh query flash in Ralph's eyes, and hurried on, 'But you don't know about that, either, do you?'

'There seems to have been a lot going on that I knew nothing about,' he remarked bitterly. 'So tell me, Tracy...tell me everything.'

I briefly explained about the letter.

'And you think,' interrupted Ralph, 'that it was Baxter who sent it?'

'I'm coming to that. The police got a list of all the people who took the magazine, and they checked up on everybody who was in the least connected with this case, to discover if any copies were missing. I was able to produce mine, and Grace showed them yours...'

'Yes, she mentioned something about being asked for it. We couldn't understand why.'

'Nothing could be solved until the missing copy was tracked down, because there were *several* not accounted for...not just Tim Baxter's. Tim had told the police that he always throws his away after glancing through it and cutting out the Cotswold Vintage advertisement. But the Haslop Hall copy had vanished, too, and Ursula Kemp's.'

Ralph, about to pour himself some more brandy, stopped with the bottle in his hand and looked at me.

'Surely,' he said, 'nobody suspected Ursula of sending an anonymous letter?'

'Well, yes. As she couldn't produce her copy of the magazine, she had to be regarded as a suspect. And there were several other things too.'

'Such as what, for heaven's sake?' He put down the brandy bottle again without pouring any.

'For a start, Ursula knew very well—because I had told her so myself—how vital the matter of timing was to me. You see, I wasn't able to bring any proof that I hadn't reached the Coach House until after twelve-fifteen that day. And if we suppose that the sender of the letter was also Oliver's murderer...'

'A big assumption!'

'Is it? The only reason for that letter must have been to divert suspicion from the real killer.'

'And was it seriously believed possible that Ursula Kemp had killed Oliver?'

'It was *me* who thought she must have done, but Neil was inclined to dismiss the idea. He was very interested in Ursula, though, because he thought she might well know something which would throw light on Oliver's death.' I sighed. It was all so terribly involved, and much of it was irrelevant now, anyway. 'You see, Ralph, it very much looked as if Oliver had been blackmailing someone.'

He made a startled exclamation. Then he demanded urgently, 'How on earth did they work out such a ridiculous theory?'

'It's not so ridiculous. You see, Oliver used to pay large sums of cash into his personal account at the bank every now and then...'

'The bloody fool!'

I stared. 'What do you mean?'

Ralph stood up abruptly and strode across the room. 'I just meant, what a fool to imagine that he could get away with blackmail. He'd be certain to be found out in the end, or...'

'Or get himself murdered,' I whispered.

'Well, yes...that's obviously what happened.' Ralph turned round to face me. 'So it was Baxter?'

'Was it?' I said slowly. All of a sudden I had been shaken with an extraordinary conviction that Neil and I were on the wrong track. I felt excitement, triumph...and at the same time a crawling sense of fear.

'Well, it *must* have been Baxter. Who else?' Ralph gave an uneasy laugh. 'Why are you looking so petrified, Tracy? You're perfectly safe. Even if Baxter spots your car outside, he won't try to follow you in here.'

I clenched my fists, desperately trying to keep calm, desperately trying to grasp a coherent line of reasoning without giving Ralph any clue as to how my brain was working.

Was this just an emotional reaction, I debated frantically; because, despite all the damning evidence stacked up against Tim, I still couldn't bear to acknowledge that he was guilty? This sudden, dizzying suspicion about Ralph...what, in truth, was it based on? Nothing more than his rather curious reaction to the suggestion that Oliver had been blackmailing someone. As though this were something that Ralph already knew about.

How, though, could I ever hope to convince Neil that it wasn't just another of my harebrained theories? Keep talking, that was all I could do now. Keep on talking to Ralph and hope that something decisive would emerge.

So, clutching at words feverishly and stringing them together, I began, 'Of course it doesn't *have* to have been Tim. I mean, it's conceivable that it could have been Ursula, after all. If Oliver had known something about her, about her past...and was blackmailing her. And, in sheer desperation, Ursula killed him.'

Ralph cut across me, 'But if they think that Ursula might have killed Oliver, then who do they imagine killed *her*?'

A sense of elation thrust through my fear. Wasn't this just what I'd wanted, a fatal slip on Ralph's part? Neil had been most insistent that Ursula's death must continue to be thought of as an accident. I had said nothing to anyone. And neither, obviously, had the police.

CHAPTER 14

I drank down the rest of my brandy, and stood up.

'Sorry to have panicked on you like that, Ralph. It was silly of me. But I feel a lot better now, so I'll be going.'

'Going where, Tracy?'

'Home, of course.'

'I thought you were terrified of Baxter,' he said.

'Well, he's obviously not followed me, has he? Besides, the police are sure to have picked him up by now.'

Ralph made a negative face. 'I can't let you take the risk. No, you'll be better off staying the night here with us.' He glanced at the french clock on the mantel. 'Grace won't be back for an hour or more, but...'

'I can't stay the night,' I protested. 'I mean, I haven't got any things with me. Besides,' I hurried on to forestall his dismissal of this objection, 'my supper is in the oven and it'll be burnt to a cinder if I leave it.'

Ralph tapped his thumbnail against his teeth

as he thought that over.

'I'll tell you what,' he said. 'I'll come to your cottage with you now, and you can turn off the oven and get some night things at the same time. Then we'll return here.'

'No honestly, there's no need...'

He interrupted me, 'I'll be much happier having you stay here. And I'm sure that Grace will be, too. She'd never forgive me if I let you out of my care, and something happened.'

'Nothing *will* happen,' I insisted.

'I insist. Now let's go.'

Outside, the village street was deserted. It was a serenely beautiful night, the thin crescent of moon floating in a cloudless sky directly above the church tower.

I drove the short distance to Honeysuckle Cottage and drew up outside.

'I won't be a minute,' I said, jumping out.

My plan was to phone Neil the instant I was inside. But to my dismay Ralph got out of the car, too, and followed me up the garden path. I didn't even have the chance to slam the front door in his face because his arm came over my shoulder, holding it open until he was inside too.

'I thought you said you'd left your supper in the oven,' he commented, sniffing the air.

Useless to pretend. With a forced little laugh,

I said, 'Well I only told you that as an excuse, Ralph, because I didn't want to put you and Grace to the trouble of having me stay the night.'

'Silly girl!'

'I...I'll just pop upstairs and collect a few things.'

He shook his head. 'Don't trouble, Tracy. D'you know, my dear, I'm thanking my lucky stars that you bumped into me this evening. Up until you spilled it all out just now, I had no idea that things were moving so fast. And so dangerously.'

I made a last attempt to bluff it out. 'I haven't the faintest idea what you're talking about, Ralph.'

'Oh, yes you have. You don't know all the details, perhaps, but enough to stop me getting away with it.'

I gave up, feeling almost a sense of relief. 'So you're admitting that it was you who killed Oliver?'

'There's not much point in trying to deny it now, is there?'

'And Ursula, too?'

He grimaced. 'I slipped up there, didn't I, letting out that I knew her death wasn't accidental. You have rather a transparent face, Tracy...fortunately.'

'But why?' I whispered in a strangled voice. 'Why did you kill them, Ralph?'

'You answered that question yourself, my dear, you and your astute young police inspector. Oliver was blackmailing me, and he did it once too often. That morning in the studio, he was demanding even more from me. And fast! It was the final straw, and I completely lost my head. The thing was done almost before I realised. When I heard your car drive into the courtyard, I wiped my fingerprints off the statuette and ran down the staircase.'

'And what about Ursula?'

'I had to kill her, too; I had no option. Stupidly, I'd let her guess that I was the one who'd killed Oliver, and she was getting squeamish. I dared not take the risk that she'd give me away.'

I stared at Ralph, sheer bewilderment to some extent overriding my fear of him.

'However did you come to let Ursula Kemp guess that you'd killed Oliver? How did she get involved in the situation?'

Ralph's face tightened. 'There's a very simple answer to that question. Kemp was an assumed name. Her real name was Ursula Ebborn.'

'Ebborn?'

'Yes. She was my wife.'

In my astonishment I took a backward step and stumbled against the bottom stair.

'You and Ursula...were once married?'

'We still were,' he said grimly. 'Ursula was my legal wife. I bitterly regret it now, but my marriage to Grace was bigamous. Ursula had left me and gone abroad, and I never expected to see or hear from her again. So it seemed pointless to cause a lot of upset for poor Grace. As you know, she's inclined to be a bit strait-laced.'

'And Oliver had somehow discovered this? That's the reason he was blackmailing you?'

'Not right at the start,' said Ralph. 'He only found out about Ursula quite recently. She let it slip out, apparently. It was that extra hold on me that made Oliver greedier than ever. He really put the screws on hard, and he got what he deserved.'

'But...but I don't understand...'

Ralph sighed. 'What does it matter, Tracy? Understanding the rest can't do a thing to help you.'

Only now, I think, did I fully understand that Ralph intended to kill me. Sick with panic, I wanted to turn and escape from him. But the only possibility open to me was up the stairs, and that would be senseless. So I desperately played for a little more time...even though I couldn't see how more time would help me.

'If...if Oliver only just found out about you and Ursula,' I stammered, 'what was he black-mailing you about before that?'

Ralph shrugged impatiently. 'He discovered that I was dipping into the various farm accounts and decided that he wanted a share. He thought it was a clever way of extracting more cash from the estate than his father was willing to allow him. So, with the two of them on my back, I had to step up the amount I was taking.'

'You mean that Ursula was demanding money from you as well as Oliver?'

'Yes, that was why I first began to help myself from the till,' he explained. 'My bitch of a wife, who had deserted me years before for another man, seemed to think that she was entitled to come back and be maintained by me. Ursula had been living in Canada with this chap, but when he died she returned to this country. She traced me here to Steeple Haslop, found that I was doing very nicely, and decided to settle down here and demand a regular income from me in exchange for not exposing my second marriage as bigamous. Rather than wreck my whole life, I paid up. It wasn't all that difficult to juggle the accounts, especially since Sir Robert was in no condition to keep a close eye on things.'

'And...and how did Oliver find out what you were doing?' I prompted.

'He happened to come into the estate office late one evening, when I was there alone making a few little adjustments to the books. Oliver Medway, damn him, might not have possessed much in the way of a business brain, but he was a cunning swine and he guessed at once what I was doing. No doubt he regarded it as quite natural that I should be feathering my own nest. It was just the sort of thing he'd have done himself, in my position.'

Ralph fell silent, choked with bitterness. I felt a curious stab of emotion which I recognised with surprise as pity. He'd made a first class job of being agent at the Haslop Hall estate, everyone agreed on that, and I could appreciate his reluctance to cheat Sir Robert. But his past life had caught up with him, and he'd been driven to it.

I'd always liked Ralph Ebborn and, apart from his recent coolness concerning Sebastian, he had always seemed fond of me. It struck me now that although he had already killed twice, he still had qualms about killing me in cold blood. Perhaps that was why he had been persuaded to talk so much. And if I were judging his frame of mind correctly, there lay my only, slender hope of escape.

The silence was shattered by the telephone bell. Ralph and I looked at one another.

'Are you expecting a call?' he asked.

'Yes,' I replied quickly. 'That'll be Neil.'

As I moved towards the phone on the hall table, Ralph put out an arm to bar my way.

'No you don't!' he said threateningly.

We stood there frozen into stillness, both of us staring at the phone. It rang ten times, then with a final ring it subsided into silence.

The interruption seemed to have changed Ralph's mood. He gave me almost a pleading look.

'I had to kill them, Tracy, can't you see that? They forced me into it, both of them. None of it would have happened if Ursula hadn't come back and held that threat over me.'

In a voice that was fraying with nerves, I said, 'Perhaps, if you were to make a clean breast of everything to the police, Ralph, they'd be sympathetic. I mean, better than being on the run for the rest of your life—which you'd have to be, because they're bound to find out about Ursula being your wife. Probably, in the circumstances, the charge would be manslaughter, and the law wouldn't be too hard on you.'

I had made a mistake and gone too far. Ralph lost his air of defeat and became brisk.

'Not a chance, Tracy. But I shall make a clean getaway, don't you worry. I've been prepared for it ever since I killed Oliver. I've been carrying my passport and several hundred quid in my wallet. I only need a few hours start—and I'll get that, all right. Nobody is going to look for you before morning, my dear, and although Grace will be worried, she won't get around to reporting my absence to the police for a while. By then, I'll have vanished.'

'Where, Ralph? Where can you possibly go?' I was playing for just a few more seconds while I readied myself for a final, desperate escape bid. On the wall of the stairs beside me hung an oval gilt-framed mirror. Mentally, without turning my head a fraction, I gauged its weight. I would need to sweep it from its hook in one swift movement.

'I've got it all worked out,' Ralph told me. 'I shall drive to the coast and get a cross-channel ferry. Then once in France I'll have the whole of Europe to lose myself in.'

While he was still speaking I launched myself, bringing up my arm and jerking the mirror of the wall and propelling it towards Ralph's head in a smooth arc. He raised his hand quickly to ward it off, but only succeeded in slightly deflecting my aim. He was struck on the side of the head, and the glass splintered into a hundred fragments. Ralph staggered backwards, muttering curses, both hands to his face. I saw blood between his fingers.

But in sending Ralph reeling against the front door I had blocked my own path of escape. I would have to push him aside, and I knew that he'd never let me get past. So I took the only other route, racing the length of the narrow hall to the garden door at the rear. A quick twist of the key and I was out. But Ralph was close on my tail.

After the bright light in the hall, it seemed pitch black out in the garden. There was no way round to the front of the cottage without climbing a six-foot wall, so I raced across the small lawn. As I ran past the old swing that hung from the pear tree, I gave the seat a tremendous shove. Ralph, close behind me now, must have caught the full impact of its return, solid oak and two inches thick. I heard him yell out with the pain of it, but he still came after me.

Aunt Verity's workshop loomed up ahead. I groped for the door handle and dodged inside. My plan was to hammer wildly on the great bronze gong, making a din which would be certain to bring people running to investigate. But I had miscalculated about one vital thing. The key to this door was on the outside. Once

I'd entered, it was too late to reach round for it, with Ralph so close on my heels.

Too late, also, to reach the gong. I'd never manage to strike it even once before Ralph overpowered me. So I abandoned the gong and dodged behind the massive wooden work bench.

The big windows and skylight let in what moonlight there was, and by now my eyes were growing accustomed to darkness. I could see Ralph's figure against the oblong outline of the open door, then it closed and I heard the key grate in the lock.

Ralph spoke breathlessly, in a sorrowful tone. 'You haven't a hope of escaping, Tracy. Surely you see that.'

'Keep away from me,' I shouted, 'or I'll...'

'You'll do what? You've got plenty of spirit, my dear, you always have had, but there's nothing more you can do to help yourself now. God knows I dislike the idea of anything so drastic, but I have to make sure that you don't get a chance to raise the alarm. So let's get it over with.'

He advanced towards me across the concrete floor. When I saw that he was circling round the end of the bench, I kept the distance between us by edging round the opposite end.

'It's no use thinking you can make a dash

for it,' he warned. 'You heard me lock the door, and I've pocketed the key.'

Despair came swamping down on me. I could try screaming my head off, but there was precious little hope that my voice would be heard. Better to conserve my energy, and my wits.

Even as it was, my attention had strayed for a vital split second. When Ralph made a sudden lunge to grab me, I only just managed to evade him. As I fled across the workshop I stubbed my toe against something loose which I realised was a wooden mallet. Bending quickly, I snatched it up and flung it back at Ralph. But it missed him, making a clatter as it fell to the floor.

I ducked behind the great block of pink alabaster—Aunt Verity's unfinished sculpture of Hebe—and it seemed for a moment that Ralph was uncertain where I'd gone. This was my single advantage over him, that I knew the layout of the workshop better than he did, so I could move about more easily in the dark. But if he found the light switches, it would be a different story.

The mallet had given me a sudden new thought. On the wall racks behind the bench were rows of sculptor's tools...hammers and wickedly sharp chisels—points and claws, my aunt had called them. If only I could get back there and snatch a couple, I'd be armed with lethal weapons.

Deliberately, I scraped the toe of my shoe across the concrete floor. The sound alerted Ralph, and he came at me with a cry of triumph. I broke free again and raced to my first retreat behind the bench. In a fever, I felt along the rows of tools and found what I wanted. Heavy steel chisels, tempered to a point. I clutched one in each hand as Ralph came after me again.

'Keep away,' I called, 'or you'll be sorry.'

Something in my tone made him pause. 'Another clever trick, Tracy? What is it this time?'

I extended one arm into a pallid glimmer of moonlight that slanted in through the side window. Perhaps he would just get a glimpse of what I held in my clenched fist.

'It's a chisel, Ralph, very sharp and very dangerous. I've got two of them! I don't want to use them, but I will if you force me to.'

I saw his shape move back a little into deeper shadow. He said, 'Don't be a fool, Tracy. You're only prolonging the agony, you know.'

'I mean it, Ralph,' I assured him. 'Look, why don't you just make a run for it? What if I promise not to alert the police for an hour…two hours, if you like…'

His voice coming out of the darkness bit me with sarcasm. 'I hope you've got your fingers crossed, Tracy, because you don't mean a word of it. You'd be on the phone to your friend Neil Grant in a minute flat.'

He was moving as he spoke, but not coming nearer. Straining my eyes I could just make out that he seemed to be stooping down across the room, over by the sink.

I had to go on lying, hoping to make him believe me. 'You're wrong, Ralph,' I insisted. 'I know that you don't want to kill me, any more than you wanted to kill Oliver and Ursula. You could still get away. I don't need to tell anyone where you'll be heading.'

Ralph grunted, as if preoccupied. He started moving again, still half crouched down, approaching my end of the bench. Warily, I took a step or two away from him, but he came no further.

'You're wasting your breath, Tracy,' he said after a moment. I saw him straighten up and stand there, as if staring at me, though I knew he could see me no more distinctly than I could see him. It seemed to be a stalemate, for the moment.

From far off I heard the drone of an engine. An airplane? No, a car. My ear detected the deepening note as it slowed to take the corner into Millpond Lane. One of my two neighbours, perhaps, or someone from the farm half a mile further on? Somehow or other, I had to catch their attention.

Twelve feet above me, the big skylight was a pale square of grey in the gloom. An easy target, surely? I weighed the heavier of the two chisels in my hand, swinging it once, twice... and then letting fly. A brief second of silence, then the night quiet was shattered by the sound of breaking glass. Broken pieces came showering down to smash again on the hard concrete floor.

The car stopped. I heard doors slam and voices shouting.

'It's all up, Ralph,' I cried with a surge of relief. Then I yelled at the top of my voice, 'Help! In the workshop. Help!'

For a moment or so Ralph seemed petrified. Then he made a sudden lunge at me. I dodged away, then spun about to face him with my remaining chisel raised to strike. But now that rescue was at hand, I couldn't bring myself to smash such a vicious weapon into his face. Ralph grabbed at me, twisted my wrist, and forced me to drop the chisel. With his arm around my neck he held me locked against him in a clamplike grip.

Outside, there were confused noises, and I saw flashes of light through the high windows. I struggled against Ralph with all my strength, but I couldn't break his hold on me.

I screamed again.

Someone shouted back. The door rattled, and a second later it shuddered from what must have been an almighty kick. Another kick. At the third try the lock gave way and the door crashed open. A flashlight beam stabbed around the workshop before it homed on the two of us, dazzling my eyes.

'Keep away,' warned Ralph, his grip on me tightening. 'Keep right away, whoever you are, or I'll...'

'We're the police, Ebborn!' It was Neil's voice. 'Let her go, man. You can't hope to get away now.'

'Listen to me, Grant...you do exactly as I say, or by God I'll break the girl's neck. I mean it!'

'Don't be a bloody fool! You'll only make it worse for yourself.'

'I told you to *listen*, Grant. Stand clear of the door, and shine the light on yourselves. How many of you are there, anyway?'

'Enough of us to deal with you,' said Neil. 'Be in no doubt of that. Give yourself up.'

From somewhere behind Neil there was a

flurry of movement and a dark shape came hurtling towards us in a flying Rugby tackle. Ralph and I were both carried down to the floor and I felt all the breath knocked out of me. I felt hands drag me free of Ralph, who took the chance to scramble to his feet and make a dash for the door. An instant later, though, he uttered a terrified shout and there was a sickening thud. Silence followed.

'Are you all right, darling?' Incredibly, it was Tim's voice, close to my ear.

'Tim! Yes...but how...?'

'Ssh! Later, not now!' Gently, he lifted me to a sitting position. 'Nothing broken?'

'No, but I...'

'Good! Then let's see what the devil has happened.'

The darkness flickered, then the banks of fluorescent tubes in the ceiling came on. Blinking, I gazed around me. Neil strode across the floor to the centre of the room, where Ralph lay crumpled in a heap at the foot of the huge block of alabaster.

'What's he done?' asked Tim. 'Knocked himself out?'

'No,' said Neil, rising to his feet.

'Then what?'

'He's killed himself.'

I gasped. 'But...how?'

270

'He fell across this trip wire and hit his head against the...'

'Trip wire?' I exclaimed in astonishment. Then suddenly I understood and gave a shudder. 'That was meant for me! I suppose Ralph found a coil of modelling wire on Aunt Verity's work bench and it gave him the idea. I couldn't make out what he was doing just now, when I saw him fiddling around in the darkness.'

'A very nasty little device,' said Neil. 'Only Ebborn copped it himself as he rushed for the door. He must have taken a headlong dive at this two-ton slab of rock.'

CHAPTER 15

I felt a burning need to bare my conscience, but Tim refused to listen to me. We were sitting on the sofa in my living room, while all kinds of people connected with the police trudged through the hallway of Honeysuckle Cottage.

'I still don't see what brought you here to the cottage, Tim. I mean, what happened after Neil's men came to the vineyard to pick you up?'

'They didn't. I reported to Neil Grant of my own free will.' He grinned and dropped a kiss on my cheek. 'When you ran out on me in such a panic, it made me realise that I'd better go to the police and come clean. I'd been crazy not to do it right at the start, of course. But it seemed so incriminating to admit that Oliver Medway and I had quarrelled that morning, just minutes before he was murdered.'

'You came back to the studio to collect your keys, didn't you? I'd worked that much out, but I got the rest wrong.'

'I can't blame you,' Tim said ruefully. 'It

was my own fault. How did you guess, though, darling?'

'It came to me this evening, when you were dangling your bunch of keys on your finger. I suddenly recalled where it was that I'd seen that silver medallion of yours before...on Oliver's desk that morning. You covered up those keys with a sheet of paper, didn't you, and then you pocketed them when I went to fetch Sir Robert? And Neil told me on the phone that you'd been seen coming out of Ursula Kemp's place on Sunday evening.'

Tim laughed dryly. 'Next time I think of giving someone a thank-you present, I'd better make sure they aren't going to be murdered the following day.'

'A thank-you present?'

'Well, a couple of weeks ago Ursula Kemp sent along some customers of hers—a wealthy Canadian couple. She'd told them about the vineyard, and they asked if they could see it. I gave them a guided tour, at least an hour of my valuable time, and they finished up ordering one miserable case of wine! Still, Ursula meant well, and I'd had it on my mind ever since that I ought to present her with a bottle as a goodwill gesture. I finally got around to it last Sunday night. After you and I packed it in early, I felt at loose ends and went along to the Trout for a drink. On the way home I saw Ursula's lights on, and I remembered that I'd got a bottle in the car left over from our picnic. So I dropped it in there and then.'

'I never for a moment thought of anything like that,' I said slowly. 'When Neil told me that you'd called on Ursula, after dark...it was all getting so complicated, I just jumped to the worst conclusion. And then that business of your wiping my fingerprints off the statuette... I'd never been entirely able to dismiss the idea that you were wiping off your own prints, Tim.' I turned to look at him. 'Why *did* you wipe the statuette?'

He touched my cheek with his fingertip. 'Do I need to answer that question?'

'But you didn't feel this way about me then,' I persisted.

'Well, I'd recently been noticing you afresh, you might say, and deciding that I very much liked what I saw. It was an impulse, I grant you, and I didn't give a thought to the possible consequences. I just knew that I didn't want you dragged through the mire because you were suspected of having killed that bastard, Oliver Medway.'

'You haven't yet explained what it was that you and Oliver quarrelled about,' I reminded him.

Neil's voice from the doorway said, *'I'll* tell you that, Tracy.' He came in and took his favourite sort of perch on my pembroke table.

'This was the story I was asked to believe,' he went on, 'when Tim came to HQ this evening and—very belatedly—offered me a "true" account of his movements on the morning of Oliver Medway's death. It didn't help him much, I can tell you, and he was still in one hell of a predicament. According to Tim, while he was having a small job done on his car at the garage in the village, he found himself with an hour to kill. So he decided to stroll across to the Coach House and have a word with Medway about a matter he'd had in mind for some time—sounding him out about his attitude towards a long-term scheme for financing the vineyard.'

I glanced at Tim. 'D'you mean, the sort of thing you were telling me about the other day?'

'Right—getting a long-term contract to tide me over if we get a run of bad-weather years. I wanted to ensure that I'd have Oliver Medway's backing, in view of the fact that he was likely to inherit the Haslop Hall estate in the not too distant future.'

'And how did Oliver react?' I asked.

Tim pulled a long face. 'I'd chosen the worst possible moment, because he was in a thoroughly bloody mood. He must have got out of bed on the wrong side.'

Cynthia Fairford's bed, as Neil knew. I could have explained to Tim that Oliver and Cynthia had quarrelled before parting that morning, but this was something Neil hadn't discovered, and I preferred to keep it that way.

'Medway saw at once how much it meant to me,' Tim went on, 'and it gave him a kick to play me like a fish on the end of a line. He said that I'd damn well have to wait and see until the time came, and that even if I negotiated a long-term agreement with his father, he'd rip it up if he was so inclined. I'm afraid I lost my temper completely, and the two of us ended up in a real shouting match. And then I walked out—overlooking the fact that I'd put my car keys down on his desk while we were talking.'

'The question I had to ask myself,' Neil said, 'was whether Tim had omitted the little detail of having first bashed Medway over the head. If we were to accept his story, then we also had to accept the fact that in the short space of time between his departure and your arriving, Tracy, someone else appeared on the scene and committed the murder. Which took a bit of believing.'

'All the same,' I said, 'that was exactly what

did happen. Ralph Ebborn killed Oliver because Oliver was blackmailing him.'

Neil scratched his eyebrow. 'You have to remember, Tracy, that we didn't have a black mark against Ebborn at that stage—or rather, we just had a single grey smudge on account of his having covered up for Sebastian Medway. But nothing against Ebborn on his own account.'

'Why, then,' I asked, 'were you so ready to accept that it was Ralph? What made you come charging out here with him to find me?'

'Because of some further information that came through while Tim was in my office. It was from the people we'd had checking up on Ursula Kemp's past.'

'They had discovered that Ursula was really Ralph Ebborn's wife, you mean?'

'So he told you about that, did he? I realised at once that somehow or other he had to be behind these murders. It would have been stretching improbability altogether too far, if not. Besides which,' he added with a grin, 'I was prejudiced in Tim's favour and wanted to believe his implausible story.'

Tim gave a short, incredulous laugh. 'You could have fooled me! I got a distinct impression that you'd like nothing better than to have me behind bars.'

'I admit,' said Neil, with a glance at me, 'that I was tempted to put you out of harm's way. But I allowed my better nature to prevail. Come to think of it, though, I could probably still dream up a minor charge or two that would get you locked up for a spell. It's not a bad idea.'

'Don't you dare,' I said.

Neil sighed. 'He's had it too bloody easy, that man, him and his showy Rugby tackle. At school, I remember, the girls on the sidelines used to swoon. My poor effort tonight didn't stand a chance...'

'I'm terribly grateful, Neil, truly.'

Neil made a most un-policemanlike remark about the value he placed upon my gratitude. Then he became brisk.

'And now for pity's sake, Tim Baxter, stop clutching the girl's hand as if you're never going to let go, and allow me to put some questions to her. I need a complete run-through of everything Ralph Ebborn told you, Tracy. Every last detail.'

'And then,' I suggested sweetly, 'you'll send Detective Sergeant Willis round here to see if he can catch me out in a discrepancy?'

'Detective Sergeant Willis is already here,' retorted Neil with a grin. 'He can come in now and save me the trouble of doing my own paperwork.' He went to the door, and called,

'Dave, bring your notebook, will you? Now then, Tracy, begin!'

Afterwards, Neil faced the task of breaking the news to Grace, and he was going to send for a female police officer to accompany him. But when I said that he could leave the whole job to me if he wished, he was grateful. Tim came with me, and I was glad to have his support.

At The Larches, we found that Grace had just arrived back from her excursion to the Shakespeare Memorial Theatre. She answered the door blithely, thinking it must be Ralph who'd gone to the pub without his latchkey.

The next few minutes were almost worse than the terrifying ordeal I'd been through this evening. Not only did I have to inform her that Ralph was dead; I also had to find words to relate the horrific deeds of this man, who—she further needed to be told—was never her lawful husband.

Up until this time, though fond of Grace, I had always been rather tickled by her overdone gentility. Now I could only admire her fortitude. She was stricken, of course, but I felt confident that Grace would survive and come through. She was a Murchison, and pride obliged her to hold her head high.

Tim stayed a little while, until I signalled for him to leave.

'I'll persuade Grace to try and get some sleep now,' I whispered to him in the narrow hall, as I showed him out. 'I'll ring you in the morning sometime. Okay?' He touched my cheek with his lips, and was gone.

Grace did sleep, fitfully, and in the morning she faced a visit from a woman police sergeant with the same admirable fortitude. I took the chance to phone Tim, and told him that I'd be staying on at the Larches, as I felt that Grace needed me.

Neil turned up in the afternoon. He spoke to Grace with great kindness, and when she insisted on going to make a pot of tea, he murmured admiringly, 'Now there's a courageous woman, Tracy.'

Grace brought in the tea and some of her home-made shortbread, then tactfully left us alone. Guessing that there were things for Neil to tell me, she said that she was going to lie down for a while.

'I've had a long session up at the Hall this morning,' he began as the door closed behind her. 'I consider that you're entitled to a few explanations, Tracy.'

'How did Sir Robert and Lady Medway take the news?' I asked.

280

He gave me a humourless smile. 'Don't misunderstand me if I say—with relief! Those two people have been living in hell. You see, each of them believed that the other one had killed Oliver. You and I were on the right track, you know, where the Medways were concerned. We couldn't have guessed, though, what it was that sparked off their quarrel that morning.'

'What was it?'

'A phone conversation that Sir Robert overheard. Lady Medway, I gathered, had carelessly left the door of her boudoir slightly ajar while she talked on the phone to Oliver, and she was ranting at him for standing her up the previous night.'

'So she and Oliver really *were...?*'

Neil nodded. 'That information didn't come easily, Tracy. I couldn't insist on Sir Robert dotting every last "i", so I've had to make a few intelligent guesses to fill the gaps. Apparently Lady Medway has always been in the habit of walking in the grounds or going for a drive at night, when she supposedly couldn't sleep. Poor old devil, you can't help feeling sorry for him.'

Neil passed a hand across his face in a weary gesture. 'Anyway, after this flaming row with his wife, Sir Robert goes stalking off round the estate, while she sets out riding. Next thing, you turn up with the news that Oliver has been murdered. To Lady Medway the explanation was crystal clear. In order to protect her husband, she tried to cloud the issue by sending us that anonymous letter about you.'

'So it was Diana Medway,' I said, not without a certain degree of satisfaction. She must have dropped it in at the Gilchester police station on one of those night drives of hers.

'It's pity about that,' remarked Neil. 'It makes the situation rather messy. From our point of view, it's the only actionable thing that either of the Medways has done. The woman must have been half demented, of course, seeing her entire world crashing down around her.'

'And all the time Sir Robert was thinking that *she* had killed Oliver?'

'That's right—out of jealousy. From what he'd overheard of the phone conversation, he surmised that Oliver had stood her up the previous night in favour of another woman— the woman being, as you and I know, Mrs Cynthia Fairford. From all I've learnt about Oliver Medway, I can imagine that he greatly enjoyed playing his women off one against the other.'

I too had learnt a lot about Oliver during the past week since his death. That bastard

Medway, Tim had called him, and he'd been right, no question. Like a horde of other women, I'd been taken in by Oliver's devastating charm. And in my case there had been a kind of hero-worship; I'd considered him a near-genius when it came to interior design. Deep down, though, perhaps I'd always recognised Oliver Medway for what he really was; otherwise wouldn't I have succumbed like all those other women?

'I think I'll pop over to the Old Rectory at Dodford later on,' I said, 'to put Cynthia's mind at rest. She must still be worried sick.'

Neil's eyes registered alarm. 'What I've just told you is for your private ear alone, Tracy.'

'Don't worry, I won't tell her anything she shouldn't know. Only that her affair with Oliver can be buried and forgotten now.' I thought for a moment, then surprised myself by saying. 'Do you really have to take action against Diana Medway over that anonymous letter?'

'What a truly forgiving nature you have, Tracy Yorke!'

'It's not so much her I'm thinking of,' I explained. 'But Sir Robert will suffer as well, if she's prosecuted. Surely it can be quietly overlooked?'

'That's not up to me, Tracy. My Chief

Superintendent...'

'Your Chief Superintendent,' I interrupted, 'can be influenced. Yes?'

His grin was a long-suffering one. 'I suppose so.'

'Good. That's settled, then. Did you find out from Sir Robert why he suddenly changed his mind and tried to persuade me to go away?'

'This is guesswork, mostly. I reckon the poor old boy felt certain you must know about his wife's affair with Oliver, and he was afraid that you would expose the fact. So his immediate thought was to placate you in the most obvious way by offering you the Design Studio. Then he panicked at the idea of your remaining in the neighbourhood, and tried a new tack. But it wasn't only fear, I'm sure. He did feel quite a sense of obligation to you for keeping his son going in a successful business venture—more than you can have guessed, Tracy. In London, so our enquiries have revealed, Oliver Medway sailed very near the wind, and it was only a matter of time before he was nabbed on some kind of fraud charge.'

I sighed. 'Will Sir Robert and Lady Medway be staying together, d'you suppose?'

'Oh yes, I should think so. The old boy needs her now; he's looking quite incredibly frail. It's my belief that the running of the estate will very shortly be passed over lock, stock, and barrel to young Sebastian, and Sir Robert and Lady Medway will live a quiet life—somewhere on the Mediterranean—that's where I'd go if I had their sort of money. Mind you, she'll be little more than his nurse, which will serve her right.'

'She'll find other amusements,' I observed.

'No doubt she will.'

'Sebastian will probably make a first-class job of running Haslop Hall,' I said, striving to be fair. 'He's got all the abilities that Oliver lacked. There's one thing, though—he'll have trouble finding an agent as good as Ralph.'

'Does a good agent dip his hand in the till?'

'Oh, Sebastian will see that it doesn't happen again,' I said confidently.

Neil settled himself more comfortably beside me on the velvet sofa. 'And what will you be doing now, Tracy?'

It was odd, but I already had things worked out neatly in my mind.

'I shan't stay at the Coach House,' I said, 'even if Sebastian would let me. Instead, I shall convert the workshop here for the Design Studio. And I'm going to offer to let Honeysuckle Cottage to Grace. She's always liked the cottage and she wouldn't want to stay in this house—neither could she afford to without

Ralph's salary. I reckon it will work out quite nicely.'

'You're a real little Miss Fix-it, aren't you?' said Neil. 'But I really meant, what about you and...Tim?'

'Oh, I'm going to marry Tim.'

'You mean that he's already got around to proposing?'

I laughed. 'Well, he's not exactly asked me to name the day. But he will, very soon.'

Neil scuffed the dove-grey carpet with the toe of his shoe.

Maybe we could ask him to be best man.

Two days later Tim and I stood together, holding hands, on the rounded top of the hillock above his vineyard. To the west, a huge crimson sun was sinking behind the distant hills.

'It'll be a good vintage this year, I reckon,' he said. Then, 'I shouldn't have any trouble with Sebastian.'

Dear Tim, thinking there was a need to sell himself to me with promises of the good life.

I had one question for him. It didn't bother me, of course, but I was still curious.

'Monday evening,' I said, 'when you were supposed to be home doing your VAT return, I rang you, but you didn't answer.'

He turned me a puzzled look. 'But I was there, Tracy.'

'I rang and rang,' I pointed out, 'for five minutes, at least.'

'What time was this?'

'I don't know. Ten-ish.'

'I remember now,' he said slowly. 'I went out for a breather, a few minutes stroll round the vineyard.'

'But the external bell?'

'I wouldn't have bothered to switch it on.'

'I wish you *had* done, Tim,' I said with a shudder. 'When Neil and I worked out that Ursula's death was no accident, and I remembered that you hadn't answered the phone....'

'Forget it, darling,' he said. 'Forget the whole thing.'

But I never would, ever.

The sun edged lower, and the entire western sky glowed crimson. Below us, Steeple Haslop was bathed in the tranquility of a lovely summer's evening.

Tim drew me closer to him. 'All those things going on,' he mused. 'Oliver and Ursula and Ralph...and none of us had a clue about it. You have to wonder what else is going on under the surface in our peaceful village.'

'It's probably a seething cauldron of intrigue,' I answered. 'But I don't want to think about that, Tim.'

His arms went around me and I leaned against him, happiness flooding through me. We kissed for long, lovely moments, and then Tim put the question that I had been expecting.

'Tracy darling, will you marry me?'